FIVE MINUTE MYSTERIES

containing
**MICHAEL STARR
INVESTIGATES**
and
**THE MEMOIRS OF
ANDRE d'ARNELL**

Francis Durbridge

WILLIAMS & WHITING

Cover design by Timo Schroeder

9781912582907

Williams & Whiting (Publishers)

15 Chestnut Grove, Hurstpierpoint,

West Sussex, BN6 9SS

Titles by Francis Durbridge published by Williams & Whiting

Murder At The Weekend – the rediscovered newspaper serials and short stories

Also published by Williams & Whiting:
Francis Durbridge : The Complete Guide
By Melvyn Barnes

INTRODUCTION

Francis Durbridge (1912-98) began his career in 1933 as a writer of sketches, stories and plays for BBC radio. They were mostly light entertainments, including libretti for musical comedies, but a talent for crime fiction became evident in his radio plays *Murder in the Midlands* (1934) *and Murder in the Embassy* (1937).

He continued to write radio plays and serials for many years, using his own name and the pseudonyms Frank Cromwell, Nicholas Vane and Lewis Middleton Harvey, but his triumph was the creation of novelist/detective Paul Temple and his wife Steve. When the serial *Send for Paul Temple* was broadcast in 1938, listeners bombarded the BBC with over 7,000 requests for more and Durbridge responded later the same year with *Paul Temple and the Front Page Men*. From 1939 to 1968 there were another twenty-six Paul Temple radio productions, of which seven were new versions of earlier cases.

Durbridge's skills were not, of course, confined to the radio. He became perhaps even better known for the fact that in 1952, while continuing to write for radio, he embarked on a sequence of BBC television serials (not featuring the Temples) that achieved huge viewing figures until 1980. Indeed the first of these, *The Broken Horseshoe* (1952), was the first thriller serial on British television – defined as a continuing story in several episodes rather than a series of separate plays. But even more can be credited to this master of mystery, as he also wrote nine intriguing and sophisticated stage plays that have been produced throughout the UK since 1971.

This volume in the Williams and Whiting series of rediscovered scripts might come as something of a surprise, however. *Michael Starr Investigates*, broadcast from 14 February to 7 August 1944, consisted of twenty-six very brief "weekly detective problems" included in the variety programme *Monday Night at Eight*. They doubtless provided a welcome diversion for listeners at a time when wartime audiences on the home front were looking for light entertainment, because Durbridge quickly followed up with *The Memoirs of Andre d'Arnell*. These nine episodes, in the same vein as the Michael Starr puzzles, were broadcast from 9 October to 27 November and 18 December 1944 and again formed part of *Monday Night at Eight*.

Henry Oscar (1891-1969), as Michael Starr, was a busy actor on stage, screen and radio who later appeared in the film version of Durbridge's television serial *Portrait of Alison* (1955). Michael Starr's "foil", Inspector McCraw, was played by the prolific radio actor Ian Sadler (1902-71), who was a genuine Scot but also adept at a range of foreign accents. Among his other Durbridge radio appearances were *Introducing Gail Carlton* (1943/44, by the pseudonymous Nicholas Vane), *Passport to Danger!* (1945), *The Caspary Affair* (1946), *Paul Temple and the Sullivan Mystery* (1947/48), *Johnny Washington Esquire* (1949) and *Mr Hartington Died Tomorrow* (New production 1950, by the pseudonymous Lewis Middleton Harvey). Sadler even had the distinction of playing the same part (Don Alfaro) in both productions of *Paul Temple and the Madison Mystery* (1949 and 1955).

In *The Memoirs of Andre d'Arnell*, playing d'Arnell's wife Lucille was Linden Travers (1913-2001). Predominantly a film actress (with credits including Hitchcock's *The Lady Vanishes* in 1938), she made occasional radio appearances and soon after her regular slots as Lucille d'Arnell she co-starred with Carl Bernard in Durbridge's radio serial *Passport to Danger!* (1945).

But Starr and d'Arnell were not the first detectives to tease radio listeners with "audience participation" mysteries in which a criminal's fatal slip was the key point, and neither were they the last. *Inspector Hornleigh Investigates* was first broadcast on 31 May 1937 as part of the variety show *Monday at Seven* (later *Monday Night at Seven*), and over one hundred of these brief puzzles ran until 27 May 1940. Written by Hans W. Priwin and starring S.J. Warmington as Hornleigh, the series might well have influenced Durbridge to turn his hand to the same sort of thing a few years later. In fact Hornleigh had more than a radio existence, as from 1938 to 1941 a trilogy of films starred Gordon Harker in the title role and Alastair Sim as his assistant Sergeant Bingham. Much later, there was even a 1961 German television series called *Inspektor Hornleigh greift ein...*, with the four episodes written by John P. Wynn. It will come as no surprise that the naturalised Wynn was born in Germany as Hans Wolfgang Priwin.

Guilty Party was another series of radio mysteries that challenged listeners to find the vital clues. Broadcast from 15 February 1954 to 23 October 1962, but this time with episodes lasting thirty minutes, the several series were written by Edward J. Mason. Although it was sub-titled "You Too Can Be A Detective", the novelty was that it also had a panel of experts - John Arlott, F.R. Buckley and former Detective Superintendent Robert Fabian – tasked with interrogating the suspects.

And so we return to John P. Wynn, who gave his 1937-40 character Inspector Hornleigh a new manifestation for a long run of thirty-minute puzzles broadcast from 5 July 1957 to 15 December 1963. *Inspector Scott Investigates* had the much-loved actor Deryck Guyler in the title role, and again his assistant was called Sergeant Bingham. This time, each play was followed by a musical interlude that enabled listeners to think of the clue that gave the criminal away.

While Durbridge's mini-mysteries featuring Michael Starr and Andre d'Arnell might not compare with his more substantial plays and serials, it is hoped that their publication for the first time will give today's readers some enjoyment and an understanding of how appropriately they fitted into the wartime radio variety shows that provided light entertainment during dark days. Sadly this volume falls slightly short of all the Francis Durbridge scripts, as one Michael Starr episode is missing from the BBC archives although the other twenty-five have survived. And please do not be frustrated by the fact that, while all of the Andre d'Arnell episodes have survived, two of them lack their concluding sections in which the solution is revealed – but do enjoy solving them for yourself!

Melvyn Barnes
Author of *Francis Durbridge: The Complete Guide* (Williams & Whiting, 2018)

This book reproduces Francis Durbridge's original script together with the list of characters and actors of the BBC programme on the dates mentioned, but the eventual broadcast might have edited Durbridge's script in respect of scenes, dialogue and character names.

MICHAEL STARR INVESTIGATES

A series of twenty-six detective problems, broadcast on the BBC Home Service from 14 February to 7 August 1944 in the weekly variety show *Monday Night at Eight*, produced by Harry S. Pepper

MYSTERY ONE
Cast:

Michael Starr . . . . Henry Oscar

Inspector McCraw . . . . Ian Sadler

Diana Donovan . . . . Rita Vale

Grace Carson . . . . Freda Falconer

James Donovan . . Preston Lockwood

OPENING MUSIC

As the music finishes CROSS FADE to the sound of a fast travelling car.

GRACE: Diana, I do wish you'd slow down – we're going far too fast!

DIANA: Nonsense! We've got to get to Town before the blackout. I don't know about you, darling, but I simply loathe driving in the dark.

GRACE: Do ... do be careful, Diana! (*Suddenly: weakly*) Oh!

DIANA: (*Amused*) My dear, you are nervous!

A slight pause.

The sound of a second car is heard.

GRACE: There's – there's a car behind us, Diana ... he wants to pass you.

DIANA: Well ... he can't pass me here ... we're almost on top of the bridge.

GRACE: Pull over, darling.

DIANA: What's he trying to do, the silly ass?

GRACE: (*Quietly*) He's – he's passing you ...

DIANA: (*Suddenly: startled*) Grace ... Grace, look who it is! Look who's driving!

GRACE: Why ... why, I never knew that he was ... (*Suddenly: desperately*) Diana! Diana, he's forcing us over ...

DIANA: My God! My God, he's going to force us over ... over the bridge! (*Tensely*) Why ... why, the swine!

GRACE: (*Terrified*) Diana!! (*Giving a startled scream*)

There is a sudden screeching of brakes and a tremendous volley of sound as the car hits the bridge: the smashing of glass, then the final crescendo as the car hits the water.

FADE

Slow FADE UP on a telephone ringing. The receiver is lifted.

STARR: Hello – this is Michael Starr speaking.

McCRAW: (*A broad Scots accent: at the moment rather excited*) Is that you, Mr Starr? Listen … this is urgent … I've got to see you!

STARR: (*Pulling McCRAW's leg*) Now don't tell me! Don't tell me! Give me three guesses … Harry Lauder? Will Fyffe? …

McCRAW: Mike … this is serious! It's no time for joking …

STARR: (*With a little laugh*) Ah! If it isn't my old friend Inspector McCraw! How are you? How are all the brilliant little boys at Scotland Yard?

McCRAW: We're not very bright, Mike – an' we want to see you!

STARR: What – now?

McCRAW: Yes – now!

STARR: Don't be silly. I've got a blonde here – a most gorgeous creature!

McCRAW: I don't care if you've got Dorothy Lamour! Dump her in the bathroom an' get down to Scotland Yard!

STARR: (*Dramatically*) Bob … I'll be with you in fifteen minutes!!

FADE

McCRAW: (*Coming in – talking swiftly*) So you see, Mike, it's no good pretending I make head or tail of it because I don't. This case has got me rattled … if it wasn't for me strong constitution I should be …

STARR: (*Interrupting McCRAW*) Yes,well supposing we skip the part about your constitution and get down to the facts. What happened? Who are the people concerned? Why? And when?

4

McCRAW: Well, two days ago a wealthy young woman by the name of Diana Donovan motored down to Ailsforth. She had a friend with her, a girl by the name of Grace Carson. On the way back someone forced the car over the bridge near Crossford and both Miss Donovan and the Carson girl were killed. No one saw the accident, but there's no doubt about it, Mike, it was murder. Murder ... pure an' simple.

STARR: M'm – had Miss Donovan any – er – relations in Town?

McCRAW: Yes – a brother. Er – James Donovan. He seems quite an amiable sort o' laddie, but I'm afraid he didn't get along very well with his sister.

STARR: Does he benefit at all by his sister's death?

McCRAW: Benefit, did ye say? Man, I should say so! He comes into about two hundred thousand ...

STARR: When did he see her last?

McCRAW: About three years ago.

STARR: Three years ago!

McCRAW: Aye, he hasn't even spoken to her for three years. He didn't even know where the lassie lived until we told him.

STARR: Where does she live, Bob?

McCRAW: At ... er ... Now where did I put that address? Oh! Here we are! (*Reading*) Miss Diana Donovan, Flat G, Henson Mansions, Kensington.

STARR: M'm – have you been through her stuff?

McGRAW: Aye, but we're going through it again tomorrow morning. Donovan's going to be there. I'm thinking he'll get quite a surprise when he sees the flat – swanky sort o' place.

STARR: What time are you meeting him?

McCRAW: Just after eleven.

STARR:	O.K. I'll pick you up at the Yard and we'll drive down together.
McCRAW:	Fine! (*With a sigh*) Well, I hope for my sake you can put your finger on the weak spot, Mike. Only last night the wife said: "Bob", she said, "if it wasn't for your strong constitution, you'd be having ...

FADE McCRAW's voice

FADE UP

McCRAW:	Ah, here's Mr Donovan now. (*Brightly*) Good morning, sir.
DONOVAN:	Good morning, Inspector. Sorry I'm late.
McCRAW:	Oh, Mr Donovan, I'd like you to meet a friend of mine – Michael Starr.
DONOVAN:	How do you do, sir?
STARR:	How do you do, Mr Donovan?
McCRAW:	Here's the lift!

We hear the opening and closing of a lift gate.

McCRAW:	I'm thinking this lift must have been made for pygmies: it certainly wasn't built for anyone with my – er – constitution.
STARR:	(*Laughing*) Wrong word, Bob – but we get the idea. (*Straining*) Can you reach the button ...
DONOVAN:	It's all right, I'll do it.

FADE IN of the lift ascending.

The lift stops.
The door opens and closes.

McCRAW:	This way, Mr Donovan! You're going the wrong way. The flat's over here.
DONOVAN:	Oh. I'm so sorry.

We hear the sound of the key fitting in the lock and the door opening.

McCRAW: Here we are.

STARR: You were certainly right about the flat, Bob.

DONOVAN: (*Impressed*) Yes! Diana certainly did herself well.

McCRAW: Well, the first thing I should like to do, Mr Donovan, is to go through …

STARR: (*Sharply*) The first thing you want to do, Bob, is to get out a warrant.

McCRAW: (*Surprised*) A warrant? For what?

STARR: (*Dramatically*) For the arrest of James Donovan!

DONOVAN: What!

STARR: You made a slip, Mr Donovan. A rather … unfortunate … slip …

A moment's pause.

DONOVAN: (*Tensely*) Oh! So you spotted it, eh? (*Suddenly*) Stand back! Well, I'm not making any more slips, Mr Clever! You see this revolver?

A tense pause.

STARR: (*Slowly, with a strange politeness*) Since it's pointing directly at my heart I could hardly fail … to … see … it, Mr Donovan.

FADE UP of music.

ANNOUNCER: Well, what made Michael Starr suspect James Donovan? Do you know? Later in the programme we shall continue the adventure and hear from Michael Starr himself the solution to tonight's problem.

MYSTERY ONE – THE SOLUTION

ANNOUNCER: We now return you to the flat for the solution to tonight's detective problem.

STARR: (*Slowly, with a strange politeness*) Since it's pointing directly at my heart I could hardly fail ... to ... see ... it, Mr Donovan. (*After a tiny pause*) But unfortunately the revolver happens to be unloaded!

DONOVAN: What!

STARR: We stood rather close together in the lift, Mr Donovan, and I took the liberty of ... (*Suddenly*) Quickly, Bob!

There is the sound of a terrific blow as STARR strikes out.

DONOVAN: Ow!!

We hear another thud.

McCRAW: Ye Gods, you've knocked him cold! But – but what on earth made ye suspect him?

STARR: Donovan said he'd never been to the flat before and yet he pressed the right button in the lift. How the devil did he know the flat was on this floor?

McCRAW: But when he got out of the lift ...

STARR: He realised what he'd done so he tried to bluff his way out of it by pretending he didn't know where the flat was. Take care of that revolver, he's waking up.

McCRAW: (*Casually*) It's all right, it's not loaded.

STARR: Oh, yes, it is.

McCRAW: What! Why, supposing he'd shot you? Or me for that matter? (*Horrified*) Why, man, he'd have blown us both to blazes!

STARR: Don't be silly. Think of your constitution!
                    (*He laughs*)

FADE UP of music.

MYSTERY TWO
Cast:
Michael Starr . . . . Henry Oscar

Inspector McCraw . . . . Ian Sadler

Wanda Mason. . . . . .Rita Vale

Georgina. . . . . Freda Falconer

Waiter . . . . .Fred Yule

Sir Gilbert Drawson . . . . . .Fred Yule

Denis Wainford . . . .John Dodsworth

As the opening music finishes CROSS FADE to WANDA
MASON reading an extract from Alice in Wonderland

WANDA: " …. and the White Rabbit blew three blasts on the trumpet, and called out, "First Witness!" The first witness was the Hatter. He came in with a teacup in one hand and a piece of bread and butter in the other."

The door bell rings in the background.

WANDA: "I beg pardon, your Majesty," he began, "for bringing these in: but I hadn't … (*WANDA hesitates*) Just a moment dear, I think there's someone at the door!

A pause.
The door opens.
Another pause, then WANDA says softly …

WANDA: What – what are you doing here? What do you want? (*Suddenly*) No! No, you can't come in! (*Softly: frightened*) Don't be a fool … put … put that revolver down … Now don't be a fool, put it down or I'll … I'll … (*Suddenly WANDA gasps: it is a gasp of sheer astonishment*)

A revolver shot is heard – then a second revolver shot.
A man laughs. It is the wild, hysterical laughter of a man who is almost out of his mind.
FADE SCENE.

FADE UP of a dance orchestra and the background noise of a fairly crowded dance floor.

STARR: Georgina, you dance like an angel!

GEORGINA: Thank you, Mr Starr. I wish I could return the compliment!

STARR: I'm afraid dancing isn't exactly my forte.

GEORGINA: What precisely is your forte, Michael?

13

STARR: I'm the best sitter-out in the county.

GEORGINA laughs.

WAITER: (*A cockney voice: faintly impudent*) I beg your pardon, sir.

STARR: Yes, what is it, Fred?

WAITER: You're wanted on the telephone, sir.

STARR: Oh!

WAITER: It's in the vestibule, Mr Starr.

STARR: Thank you. (*Aside to GEORGINA*) I shan't be long, darling.

FADE orchestra to the background.

STARR: (*On the phone*) Hello … Michael Starr speaking.

McCRAW: (*On the other end of the line: anxiously*) Hello, is that you, Mike?

STARR: Good heavens, if it isn't Inspector McCraw!

McCRAW: (*Urgently*) Mike, listen … jump into a taxi and get down to Scotland Yard.

STARR: Don't be silly, old boy. I'm having a night out. I've got my sister with me.

McCRAW: (*Astounded*) Your sister!

STARR: Well – er – she's acting like a sister.

McCRAW: Mike, listen … this is urgent … devilishly urgent … it's about the Mason murder!

STARR: The Mason murder? (*After a moment, quietly*) O.K., Inspector. I'll be with you in twenty minutes.

The receiver is replaced.

A pause.

STARR: (*Calling*) Oh, Fred!

WAITER: Yes, sir?

STARR: You see that lady in the corner?

WAITER: Why, yes, sir. Quite an eyeful, sir, if I may say so!

STARR: Yes, well – give the eyeful my compliments and tell her I've been called away on urgent business.

WAITER: (*After an impudent whistle*) Must be pretty urgent!

FADE UP of dance orchestra.
FADE SCENE.

FADE IN of McCRAW speaking.

McCRAW: … Well, I suppose you've read all about the Mason murder, so there's no need for me to give you the – er – full details o' the case but what I should like to do, Mike, is to …

STARR: Start at the beginning, Bob! Every newspaper seems to have carried a different version of the story.

McCRAW: Start at the beginning, do ye say? Ah! If only I knew where the beginning was, laddie, then I might be able to make head or tail o' things. However … last night, some time between 6.30 and 8 o'clock a woman by the name of Wanda Mason was murdered. Wanda Mason was a widow and she lived in a flat just off Park Lane. According to all accounts she was …

STARR: (*Interrupting McCRAW*) Did anyone visit Mrs Mason last night?

McCRAW: No, although the janitor seems to think a man entered the building at about half-past seven. We broadcast a brief description of the man in the nine o'clock news but – er – beyond bringing Sir Gilbert Drawson down on us like a cart load o' bricks it doesn't seem to have had any particular effect.

STARR: Sir Gilbert Drawson? You mean the financier?

McCRAW: Yes.

STARR: But where does he come into the picture?

McCRAW: He was a friend of Mrs Mason's. He heard the broadcast last night and when I got to the Yard this morning he was waiting for me on the doorstep! Ye know the type! Pompous as hell and full of his own importance!

STARR: (*Quietly*) Has Drawson an alibi?

McGRAW: An alibi? Sir Gilbert Drawson? Good heavens man, yes! A fool proof alibi! Don't start barking up the wrong tree, Mike! The man we suspected is a chappie by the name of Wainford … Denis Wainford.

STARR: Why do you suspect Wainford?

McCRAW: Because on Mrs Mason's death he inherited a large block of shares in the Trans-Arford Oil Combine.

STARR: The Trans-Arford Oil Combine? But isn't Sir Gilbert the Chairman of the T.A.O.C.?

McCRAW: Yes. And from all accounts he's been trying to get control of the Mason shares, but Mrs Mason refused to sell. Oh, Drawson's quite frank about it.

STARR: I suppose you don't happen to know whether Wainford intends to sell out or not?

McCRAW: I should think it's highly probable. He seems quite friendly with Drawson.

STARR: M'm – then if one accepts the theory that Sir Gilbert knew that Wainford would be willing to sell, that – er – more or less provides Drawson with a motive, doesn't it?

McCRAW: Aye … aye, I suppose it does, if you look at it like that.

The door opens.

McCRAW: Ah, here is Sir Gilbert and Mr Wainford.

16

DRAWSON:	(*Pompously, but rather a quick speaker*) Well, Inspector, I've just been having a word with the Assistant Commissioner. I've told him quite frankly that I'm not going to tolerate incompetence over this affair. Mrs Mason was a friend of mine, a very close friend, and if the description I heard over the radio last night was the only piece of concrete evidence that Scotland Yard have so far been able to ... (*Suddenly*) Oh! Oh, I don't think we've met, sir?
STARR:	My name is Michael Starr.
DRAWSON:	Oh, yes. I've heard of you, Mr Starr. Think you can help us over this affair, eh?
STARR:	I shall do my best, Sir Gilbert. But I should rather like to get things straightened out. This, I presume, is Mr Wainford?
DRAWSON:	Oh, yes. Oh, yes – so sorry. Denis Wainford – Mr Michael Starr.
STARR:	Did you see Mrs Mason last night, Mr Wainford?
WAINFORD:	(*Nervously: almost a stutter*) Good – good heavens, no. I haven't seen Mrs Mason for ... for weeks.
DRAWSON:	Same here.
McCRAW:	Sir Gilbert was in Leamington, Mike. He came back on the 8.55.
STARR:	I see. And you, Mr Wainford?
WAINFORD:	I – I went to the theatre. The – er – The Lyric. It was a charity show.
STARR:	And after the theatre?
WAINFORD:	I – I went straight home. I was rather fortunate; I picked up a taxi.
STARR:	Do you live in Town?

WAINFORD:	Richmond. I have a small bungalow not far from the … er … the Star and Garter.
STARR:	I see. (*Suddenly*) Sir Gilbert, you say you left Leamington on the 8.55?
DRAWSON:	That's right.
STARR:	What time did it get in?
DRAWSON:	Well, the train was actually due in at 11.40 but the confounded thing was nearly an hour late.
STARR:	I see.

A pause.

McCRAW:	Well – what do we make of things, Mike?
STARR:	(*Quietly*) Wanda Mason was murdered. Murdered by a homicidal maniac.
McGRAW:	(*Impatiently*) Yes! Yes, we know that. That's already been established.
STARR:	Yes – and something else has been established too, Inspector.
McGRAW:	What?
STARR:	It's been established that the man who murdered Wanda Mason is here …
DRAWSON:	Here!
McCRAW:	What d'you mean?
WAINFORD:	Here?
STARR:	Here … in … this … very … room, gentlemen!!!

FADE UP of music.
FADE DOWN.

| ANNOUNCER: | Who Murdered Wanda Mason? Do you know? Later in the programme we shall continue the adventure and hear from Michael Starr himself the solution to tonight's problem. |

Turn over to read the solution to mystery two.

MYSTERY TWO – THE SOLUTION

ANNOUNCER: We now return you to Scotland Yard for the solution to tonight's detective problem.

STARR: Here … in … this … very … room, gentlemen!!!

WAINFORD: Why – why that's nonsense!

STARR: I don't think it is nonsense, Mr Wainford! (*Sharply*) Don't you agree, Sir Gilbert?

DRAWSON: (*Suddenly: tensely*) Stand back!! Stand back, or I'll blow your rotten brains out!! (*With a sinister laugh*) Thought you were clever … thought you were very clever, didn't you? Well, I'll prove whether you're clever or not you swine, I'll … (*Suddenly*) Ow!!!!

A thud as DRAWSON hits the floor.

STARR: Nice work, Robert, my boy!

McCRAW: Nice work be blowed, I've busted my favourite inkpot –

WAINFORD: But – but, Mr Starr, what on earth made you suspect Sir Gilbert?

McCRAW: (*Bewildered*) Aye, what the devil made ye suspect Drawson?

STARR: (*Laughing*) Oh, Bob, don't be such a chump! How the devil can a man be in two places at the same time?

McCRAW: What – what do you mean?

STARR: My dear Inspector, how could Sir Gilbert Drawson have heard your announcement in the nine o'clock news if at nine o'clock he was travelling on the 8.55 from Leamington!

McCRAW: (*Surprised*) By George, I never thought of that!

WAINFORD: (*Same tone*) By George, neither did I!

STARR: (*Same tone*) By George … I think it's about time I got back to Georgina!

FADE UP of music.

MYSTERY THREE
Cast:

Michael Starr . . . . Henry Oscar
Inspector McCraw . . . . Ian Sadler
Trevor . . . . .Fred Yule
Hanson . . . . .Arthur Ridley
Frida Thompson . . . . .Freda Falconer

As the opening music finishes CROSS FADE to the sound of a motor car travelling through a fairly heavy storm.
There is a background of thunder and rain.
The car slows down and draws to a standstill.
The car door opens and closes.
FADE background noises.
A door is opened.

STARR: (*Rather hurried*) Is this the Northdell Golf Club?

TREVOR: (*Anxiously: with a faint Welsh accent*) Yes, this is it, sir. I suppose you'll be Mr Starr?

STARR: Yes. There's a storm coming up.

The door shuts.

TREVOR: There's a lot of thunder about. (*Obviously rather flustered*) We've been expecting you, sir. Inspector McCraw's in the lounge, sir. This way, sir, if you don't mind. Mind the aspidistra, sir.

STARR: I had a frightful job finding this place.

TREVOR: I expect you did, sir. It is rather out of the way. (*Suddenly*) Oh, er – my name's Trevor, sir … John Trevor. I'm the Pro here.

STARR: Oh, I see.

A door opens.

TREVOR: Mr Starr's arrived, Inspector.

McCRAW: Ah! So here you are, Mike. What the devil's detained ye?

TREVOR: I'll leave you two together, sir.

Unfortunately, the next sixteen lines of dialogue are missing.

McCRAW: After I found it? No one even saw it, laddie. I took it straight down to the local station.

STARR: M'm – what about a motive, Bob?

McGRAW: A motive! So far as I can gather everybody in the club had a motive! I think Campbell Foster was just about the most unpopular laddie I've ever heard of.

STARR: Who's the Secretary here?

McCRAW: A fellow called Hanson. He's in the bar now if you'd like to have a word with him.

STARR: Yes, I think it might be quite a good idea.

McCRAW: (*Amused*) You'll like the barmaid, Mike. Just your type. A regular blonde bombshell!

The door opens.

FADE IN HANSON and FRIDA THOMPSON talking.

HANSON: (*Rather a quiet type*) ... I knew there was something different about you, Frida. You've changed your hair style.

FRIDA: Yes. I did intend having it up; you know, perched on the top like Dorothy ...

HANSON: (*Suddenly*) Oh, hello, Inspector!

McCRAW: Mr Hanson, I'd like you to meet a friend of mine – Michael Starr.

HANSON: Oh, I'm glad to meet you, Mr Starr! (*Seriously*) Well, Inspector – any further developments?

McCRAW: (*Cautiously*) No. No, I don't think so.

FRIDA: (*Suddenly – emphatically*) Well, whoever did it – good luck to him – that's what I says!

STARR: (*Pleasantly*) I take it Mr Campbell Fraser wasn't exactly a friend of yours, Miss ...?

FRIDA: Thompson!

STARR: ... Miss Thompson?

FRIDA: A friend of mine, did you say? He certainly wasn't. I don't wish anybody any harm but ... well Foster was a rotter an' there's no getting away from it.

HANSON: (*Quietly – hesitantly*) Yes, I'm afraid Foster made life rather unbearable for quite a number of people. I'm not a man for bearing malice but ...

26

well, quite frankly, I can't see myself shedding any tears over Mr Foster. (*Suddenly*) Oh, I beg your pardon, sir – would you like a drink?

STARR: Well, I think I should rather like half a tankard of mild.

HANSON: Splendid. Inspector?

McCRAW: Nothing for me, thank you, sir.

FRIDA: Half o' mild?

HANSON: That's right, Frida. (*After a moment*) Er – forgive me if I'm speaking out of turn, Inspector, but I'm a ... (*Little laugh*) ... bit of an amateur detective myself you know, and it seems to me that if someone crept up behind Foster when he was actually in the bunker then ...

McCRAW: (*Sharply*) Who told you that?

HANSON: (*Quietly – surprised*) What? About Foster ... being ... in the bunker? Why – Why Trevor! Good Lord, I say ... I hope I haven't put my foot in it?

STARR: No, there's no reason why you shouldn't know, Mr Hanson. It'll pretty soon be common gossip.

FRIDA: Yes, an' if you asks me, bashing his head in with a niblick was too good for the swine! If I'd 'ave 'ad my way I'd ...

HANSON: (*Quietly*) That's enough, Frida! Get Mr Starr his drink. (*After a moment: softly*) I'm afraid there's a certain amount of justification for her outburst, Inspector. Foster was, well ... to say the least ... rather an unpleasant customer.

McCRAW: Aye, we gathered that.

STARR: Did you see Foster this afternoon, sir?

HANSON: Me? Good heavens no! You don't get me playing in this weather, sir. As a matter of fact I only popped in to have a word with Trevor.

STARR: I see.

HANSON: Ah, well – I'll be making a move. You have my telephone number, Inspector, if you want to get in touch with me?

McCRAW: Yes. Yes, thank you, sir.

HANSON: Goodbye, Mr Starr. Glad to have met you.

STARR: Goodbye, sir.

The door closes.

McCRAW: He seems quite an amiable sort o' laddie.

STARR: (*Quietly*) Yes.

FRIDA: Here's your drink, sir.

STARR: Oh, thank you.

FRIDA: I'm – I'm sorry about that outburst just now, sir, but …

STARR: That's all right.

STARR tosses a coin on the counter.

STARR: Keep the change!

FRIDA: Oh, thank you, sir.

STARR: Well, Bob, your very good … (*He hesitates*)

McCRAW: (*Quickly*) What is it?

STARR: (*After a tiny pause: softly*) I think there's someone listening … at the door. Wait here!

The door opens.

A long pause.

The door closes.

McCRAW: Well?

STARR: No. No, there was no one there. Damn funny, I could have sworn I heard something. Ah, well. Your very good health, Inspector! Cheerio!

McCRAW: (*After a moment: seriously*) I don't know whether you'd like to see the spot where Foster was murdered, Mike, but if you do then …

STARR: No. No, I hardly think that's necessary. After all, we now know who murdered Foster so why …

McCRAW:	(*Bewildered*) We … now … know … who … murdered … him?
STARR:	(*Pleasantly*) Why, yes. Yes, of course.
McCRAW:	But – but who did murder Foster?
STARR:	(*Politely*) Shall we tell him, Miss Thompson?
FRIDA:	(*Suddenly*) Don't move!
McCRAW:	My God!! My God, she's got a gun!
FRIDA:	Don't move! Don't move or I'll – I'll let you have it! (*A tiny pause*) You spotted the slip I made, didn't you, Mr Starr? Oh, yes. Oh yes … I knew that as soon as I'd made it. But you're not so clever, Mr Starr. Oh, no! (*She laughs*) There's … something … you've … overlooked …
STARR:	(*Quietly*) What do you mean?
FRIDA:	(*Politely*) Did you … enjoy … your drink?
McCRAW:	(*Tensely*) What – what was the matter with his drink?

A tiny pause.

FRIDA:	It – was – poisoned.
McCRAW:	My God!! Poisoned!!
FRIDA:	(*Quietly*) Michael Starr … you've got ten minutes to live!!!

FADE UP of music.

FADE DOWN.

ANNOUNCER:	Well, what made Michael Starr suspect Frida Thompson? And what is going to happen to Michael Starr? Listen to the solution later in the programme.

MYSTERY THREE – THE SOLUTION

ANNOUNCER: We now give you the solution to tonight's detective problem.

McCRAW: My God!! Poisoned!!

FRIDA: (*Quietly*) Michael Starr ... you've got ten minutes to live!

STARR: Don't be silly, old girl. Why do you think I went out into the corridor?

McCRAW: (*Puzzled*) Because you thought you heard someone at the door?

STARR: Of course I didn't hear anyone at the door! I went into the corridor to get rid of the drink. It's in the aspidistra.

McCRAW: Well, I'm damned! (*Suddenly*) Look out!

A shot is heard followed by a struggle.

STARR: O.K. Bob?

McCRAW: (*Briskly*) Yes ... Yes, I'm o.k. I've got the revolver. Oh, ye Gods – she's fainted. (*Suddenly*) Mike, what the devil made ye suspect the woman?

STARR: How did she know Foster had been killed with a niblick? Even Trevor only knew it was a golf club. He didn't know what kind!

McCRAW: Holy smoke, why yes!

STARR: (*Tensely – a sudden thought*) I say, Bob ...

McCRAW: (*Keyed up*) Yes?

STARR: I was just thinking ...

McCRAW: (*Tensely*) Yes?

STARR: ... There's an awful lot to be said for brunettes.

FADE UP of music.

30

MYSTERY FOUR
Cast:
Michael Starr . . . . Henry Oscar
Inspector McCraw . . . . Ian Sadler
Roy Nelson . . . . Lewis Stringer
Barbara Fielding . . . . .Freda Falconer
Mr Coogan . . . . .Dick Francis
Waiter . . . . .Dick Francis

As the opening music finishes CROSS FADE to the sound of a motor car.

The car draws to a standstill.

A car door opens and closes.

BARBARA: (*Tensely: obviously unhappy*) Well, goodnight … Roy.

NELSON: Goodnight, Barbara, I'm … I'm sorry this had to happen.

BARBARA: If – if that's how you feel about things there's – there's nothing more to be said.

NELSON: Shall I … take you inside?

BARBARA: No …

NELSON: You won't be frightened? I mean … it's always rather dark on the top corridor, and …

BARBARA: There's not much point in my being frightened now, is there, Roy? I've – I've got to learn to take care of myself.

NELSON: (*Softly*) I'm sorry, Barbara.

BARBARA: (*Obviously upset*) Goodnight!

FADE noise of the car.

CROSS FADE to the sound of a lift.

The lift stops.

The lift gate opens.

A slight pause.

BARBARA: (*Suddenly: tensely*) Who's there? Who's that standing by the door? What – what do you want? (*Desperately*) Take – take your hands off me! (*Suddenly: terrified*) Take – your – hands – off – me!!!

BARBARA gives a wild, almost terrified scream, then it becomes a low soft groan. She is obviously in pain.

FADE SCENE.

CROSS FADE to the sound of a dance orchestra and people dancing.

FADE DOWN slightly to the background.

McCRAW: Waiter!

WAITER: Yes, sir?

McCRAW: You see that gentleman over there; the one dancing with the blonde young lady?

WAITER: (*Surprised*) Mr Michael Starr, sir? Why, yes, sir!

McCRAW: Well, will ye be good enough to tell Mr Starr I'd like to see him. I'll be in the lounge.

WAITER: Yes, sir. Your name, sir?

McCRAW: Inspector McCraw.

WAITER: Very good, sir.

BRING UP the dance orchestra and FADE SCENE.

FADE IN of MICHAEL STARR.

STARR: ... What's the big idea, Robert, my lad! This is the second time you've ...

McCRAW: (*Interrupting STARR*) Mike! Mike! I'm in a quandary! I'm sorry if I've interrupted a tete-a-tete, but ...

STARR: I say, sit down! Take it easy! You look done in!

McCRAW: I feel done in! I've been at it since four o'clock this morning. Four o'clock, Mike! If it wasn't for me strong constitution I don't know what I'd ...

STARR: (*Interrupting McCRAW*) What is it: the Fielding murder?

McCRAW: Aye.

STARR: I read the report in The Evening Post. Seems rather a complicated affair.

McCRAW: Well, it's complicated in a simple sort o' way, if you follow me.

STARR: (*Amused*) I don't.

McCRAW: Well … a girl by the name of Barbara Fielding was engaged to a young architect called Roy Nelson. Last night Nelson broke off the engagement. He took Barbara back to her flat and, according to his story, he left her there at about a quarter to twelve. Just after three o'clock this morning the janitor started to make his usual tour o' the building: (*He hesitates*) he found Miss Fielding near the lift on the fourth floor. She was dead. (*After a moment*) Stabbed to death.

STARR: Stabbed?

McCRAW: Aye … poor lassie. She wasn't a very pretty sight, Mike.

STARR: Have you tested the knife: for fingerprints, I mean?

McCRAW: I'm afraid we haven't found the knife, Mike.

STARR: Oh. Oh, I see. What about a motive?

McCRAW: Well, there doesn't seem to be any doubt about the motive. Her flat was ransacked. So far as we can gather about four hundred pounds worth of jewellery's disappeared.

STARR: M'm – it appears that Miss Fielding said goodnight to her fiancé – or rather her ex-fiancé – took the lift to the fourth floor and came face to face with …

McCRAW: Face to face with the swine who murdered her. (*With a sigh*) Aye.

STARR: Where did Nelson leave Miss Fielding?

McCRAW: At the front entrance.

STARR: What do you mean – the front entrance? You mean the front entrance to the block of flats?

McCRAW: Aye.

STARR: So there's another way into the building?

35

McCRAW: Aye, there's a sort o' tradesman's entrance at the back o' Calthorpe Street.

STARR: (*Suddenly*) I'd like to have a chat with Nelson, Bob.

McCRAW: Well, he's still at the flat. I sent for him straight away. (*Anxiously*) I wish ye would see him, Mike.

STARR: I'll get my things. (*Suddenly*) Oh, er – Bob!

McCRAW: Yes?

STARR: (*Slowly*) How much does Roy Nelson actually know about all this?

McCRAW: (*Puzzled*) What d'you mean?

STARR: Did he see the body?

McCRAW: No. No one's seen the body except the janitor, Superintendent Bradley, and meself ... o' an' o' course the police surgeon.

STARR: M'm ...

McCRAW: We've got pretty quiet about the whole business: the newspaper report didn't even say she was stabbed ye know.

STARR: Does Nelson know that she was stabbed?

McCRAW: Aye, the police surgeon told him. I'm afraid Nelson's in rather a bad way with himself. In fact I should be rather surprised if ye don't experience a little difficulty getting any ...

FADE McCRAW's voice.

FADE UP ROY NELSON speaking.

NELSON: (*Terribly nervous and emotional*) I'm ... I'm terribly sorry there's ... there's nothing more I can tell you. We – we had rather a row and then I ... I brought Barbara home ...

STARR: Was Miss Fielding upset?

NELSON: Yes. Yes, of course ... she ... was upset.

STARR: What made you break off your engagement?

NELSON: (*Annoyed*) That's – that's rather a personal question, isn't it?

STARR: (*Quietly: rather pleasant*) All right, Mr Nelson. We won't be personal.

NELSON: Oh! Oh, I didn't mean to be rude, but …

McCRAW: Ah, here's Mr Coogan!

COOGAN: (*An elderly Hebrew*) Hello, Inspector. Any further developments?

McCRAW: I'm afraid not, sir. Oh, I'd like you to meet Mr Starr. (*To STARR*) Mr Coogan is in charge here, Mike, he's the sort o' general manager.

COOGAN: I'm pleased to meet you, Mr Starr. But I wish we were meeting under happier circumstances. Oh, a dreadful business to be sure.

STARR: How long had Miss Fielding been a tenant of yours, Mr Coogan?

COOGAN: Now let me see … oh, I should say about six or seven years.

NELSON: Barbara came here in 1936 … March … 1936 … (*Emotionally*) Poor … poor Barbara … (*Suddenly*) I'd like to get my hands on the swine who killed her! (*Tensely*) I'd stab him! I'd stab the rotten life out of him!

COOGAN: (*Quietly*) Mr Nelson, please.

McCRAW: (*Gently*) Ye want to take it easy, laddie.

NELSON: I'm – I'm all right …

COOGAN: (*Thoughtfully*) Inspector, I've been thinking …

McCRAW: Yes?

COOGAN: Once you find the knife, and take a record of the fingerprints, then surely it should be a fairly simple matter for …

STARR: But supposing there aren't any fingerprints?

COOGAN: What do you mean?

STARR:	Well, the murderer might have been very careful, Mr Coogan. He might, for instance, have ...
NELSON:	(*Interrupting STARR*) ... worn gloves?
STARR:	(*Politely*) Exactly, Mr Nelson. He might have worn gloves.
McCRAW:	Aye, well I've got a nasty sort o' feeling that we shan't find the knife. An' I've also got a nasty sort o' feeling that this is going to be one o' the unsolved mysteries of Scotland Yard.
STARR:	(*Imitating McCRAW's accent*) Then I should get rid o' your nasty sort o' feeling, Bob. (*A moment's pause: seriously*) Because there's no doubt about ... who murdered ... Barbara Fielding.
McCRAW:	(*Staggered*) You mean ... you know ... who ... murdered ... her?
STARR:	(*Quietly*) Yes. Yes, I know, Inspector. (*Politely*) Will you have a cigarette, Mr Nelson, - it'll soothe your nerves ...

FADE UP of music.

FADE DOWN.

| ANNOUNCER: | Who murdered Barbara Fielding? Do you know? Later in the programme you will hear from Michael Starr himself the solution to tonight's detective problem. |

See over for the solution to the mystery of who killed Barbara Fielding.

MYSTERY FOUR – THE SOLUTION

ANNOUNCER: We now give you the solution to tonight's detective problem.

STARR: Yes. Yes, I know, Inspector. (*Politely*) Will you have a cigarette, Mr Nelson – it'll soothe your nerves.

COOGAN: Mr Starr! Mr Starr, are we given to understand that you ... that you actually know who ... who murdered Miss Fielding?

STARR: Yes. You see, Mr Coogan, the man who murdered Barbara Fielding made a slip ... a rather unfortunate slip!

COOGAN: (*Nervously*) What – what do you mean?

STARR: You knew that Miss Fielding had been stabbed but ... how ... did ... you ... know ... that ... the ... knife ... was ... missing ...?

COOGAN: Why, you devil, I'll ...

McCRAW: Look out!!

NELSON: Oh, no you don't!

There is a terrific blow followed by a heavy thud.

STARR: (*After a moment*) Phew! That was quite a wallop, Mr Nelson. You've knocked him cold!

McCRAW: (*Surprised*) Cold?

STARR: Yes, stone cold. Bob!

McCRAW: (*Almost concerned*) The laddie can't have a very strong constitution!

FADE UP of music.

MYSTERY FIVE
Cast:
Michael Starr . . . . Henry Oscar
Inspector McCraw . . . . Ian Sadler
Rex Watford . . . . .Fred Yule

As the opening music finishes CROSS FADE to a railway train drawing into a small wayside station: carriage doors are heard opening and closing.

STARR: So here you are, you old rascal!

McCRAW: (*Out of breath*) So you've made it, Mike! Ah, splendid! Here, let me take that case!

STARR: It's all right – I can carry it! But what's all the excitement about?

McCRAW: Excitement? There's no excitement, man! I'm just a wee bit out o' breath. I thought I should miss the train. (*With a sigh of relief*) Ah – I made it though ... thanks to an excellent constitution!

STARR: Bob ...

McCRAW: Yes, Mike?

STARR: It's taken me four hours in an extremely stuffy, overheated, dusty, dirty, evil-smelling ...

McCRAW: (*Interrupting STARR*) I know! I know! But it's nice to see you, Mike! (*Pleasantly*) Did ye bring your golf clubs?

STARR: I did NOT bring my golf clubs! I came down here in answer to your telegram, and if you think that I'm going ...

McCRAW: There's a seat over here, laddie ... Come an' sit down an' I'll tell ye all about it.

In the background an occasional thrush can be heard: it is a quiet country scene.

McCRAW: Ah ... that's better ... Will ye have some 'baccy or ...

STARR: No. No, I've got a cigarette ...

McCRAW: Well, I came down here to King's Risborough about four days ago. This seemed a likely sort o' spot. There's quite a good golf club, a pretty average sort o' pub an' – if ye don't mind

43

trespassing – a fairly decent spot o' fishing. Well, I was quite enjoying myself, Mike, until … Tuesday afternoon – that was the day before yesterday.

STARR: What happened exactly on … Tuesday afternoon?

McCRAW: Well, a farm worker – chappie by the name o' Joseph Harper – had an accident. He was ploughing a field over on the other side o' the village. The tractor went too near a ditch … Harper lost his nerve … overbalanced … and was killed.

STARR: Did anyone see the accident?

McCRAW: Aye! His boss saw it. A farmer by the name of Rex Watford. Watford was apparently doin' a spot o' hedging about two or three hundred yards away. He heard Harper shout … dashed across the field … but when he got to the ditch the poor devil was already dead. (*After a moment – dubiously*) At least, that's his story …

STARR: What do you mean?

McCRAW: I don't like Watford, Mike. He's a sly, deceitful sort o' chap an' – I'm rather suspicious of him. What's more he had a motive: a motive for wanting Harper out o' the way.

STARR: M'm … have you moved the tractor?

McCRAW: Nothing's been moved, Mike – except Harper o' course. I've even had the spot marked out in the ditch where Harper fell, just in case you'd like to see it.

STARR: Yes. Yes, I would like to see it. And I'd rather like to meet Watford as well.

44

McCRAW: Well, I said we might stroll over there at about three o'clock. It's only about a quarter of a mile from the Inn. I've booked ye a room at the Inn, Mike, so there's no need for ye to …

FADE VOICE.

FADE IN MICHAEL STARR speaking.

STARR: Yes. Yes, I can see where Harper tried to turn the tractor round and I can see where he … (*Suddenly*) Mr Watford, where were you exactly when the accident happened?

WATFORD: I've already told the Inspector where I was. I was over on t'other side of the four acre …

STARR: (*Thoughtfully*) M'm – how long had Harper actually been ploughing here?

WATFORD: He started at ten in the morning. Kicked off an' 'ad a bit o' dinner at one, an' then started again just after two. The accident 'appened at about a quarter to four.

STARR: Did he stop at all during the afternoon?

WATFORD: No, he was at it all the time.

STARR: I see. So – correct me if I'm mistaken – the tractor was working all the time, without a break, from just after two o'clock in the afternoon until the time of the accident at approximately a quarter to four?

WATFORD: That's right.

STARR: You're certain of that?

WATFORD: Of course I'm certain. I could both see an' 'ear the blessed thing.

STARR: Right. Thank you, Mr Watford.

WATFORD: What about moving the tractor, Inspector? I've got a field that needs discing an' another that ought to be ploughed before the week's out!

McCRAW: Aye! Aye, that's all right.

STARR: I expect it'll take a bit of starting – it's stone cold.

WATFORD: Not it! She'll start like a bird. One swing an' … we're … off!

The tractor starts up.

McCRAW: Aye, ye can certainly swing it, Mr Watford.

WATFORD: It's more a knack than anything else, Inspector. Well …

WATFORD opens the throttle.

WATFORD: (*Shouting*) Good day to you. gentlemen!

McCRAW: (*Shouting*) Goodbye, sir!

FADE SCENE on the tractor.

FADE IN of McCRAW speaking.

McCRAW: Are ye sure ye won't have some more coffee, Mike?

STARR: No. No, thank you.

McGRAW: Ye seem strangely silent, laddie … what's troubling ye?

STARR: Oh, I was just thinking of … Mr Watford.

McCRAW: Did ye like him?

STARR: No. No, I can't say I exactly liked him, Bob. He seems very self-possessed.

McCRAW: Aye. (*Curiously – softly*) I tell you what I noticed, Mike …

STARR: Yes?

McCRAW: Did ye notice he didn't switch the tractor <u>on</u> before he started it, I mean?

STARR: The tractor was already switched on, Bob. Don't forget it hadn't been touched since the accident and at the time of the accident it didn't switch itself off, it just …

McCRAW: Konked out?

STARR:	Exactly.
McCRAW:	M'm … (*A pause – quietly*) Mike?
STARR:	Yes?
McCRAW:	What d'you think? Was Harper murdered or … was … it … just … an accident?

A pause.

| STARR: | (*Quietly*) He was murdered. |
| McCRAW: | (*Elated*) I knew it! I knew it! *(Softly – a bewildered manner)* But, Mike … how do ye know? |

FADE UP music.

FADE DOWN.

| ANNOUNCER: | How does Michael Starr know that Rex Watford murdered Joseph Harper? Later in the programme you will hear from Michael Starr himself the solution to tonight's detective problem. |

MYSTERY FIVE – THE SOLUTION

ANNOUNCER: We now return you to Michael Starr for the solution of tonight's detective problem.

STARR: (*Quietly*) He was murdered ...

McCRAW: (*Elated*) I knew it! I knew it! (*Softly – a bewildered manner*) But, Mike ... how do ye know?

STARR: Bob, listen ... and listen very carefully. When you first start a tractor up you run it on petrol. You run the tractor on petrol for probably five or six minutes to get the engine warm and then you switch over to paraffin. Is that clear?

McCRAW: Aye.

STARR: Well, according to Watford, Harper was ploughing from just after two o'clock until the time of the accident at a quarter to four. An hour and three quarters! An hour and three quarters, Bob! Don't you see? The tractor wouldn't be running on petrol, it'd be running on paraffin.

McCRAW: Aye! So, if it was an accident, when the tractor konked out at the ditch it would be switched ...

STARR: It would be switched over to paraffin ... yes! But it wasn't switched over to paraffin, Bob. Oh, no! It was switched over to petrol! You saw Watford start the tractor this afternoon. The tractor hadn't been touched and yet it started like a bird. You can't start a stone cold tractor on paraffin, Bob – whatever your constitution!

48

McCRAW:	(*Tensely*) But what do ye think happened?
STARR:	(*Eager – working up*) I'll tell you what happened. Harper started ploughing – he was interrupted by Watford. He stopped the tractor. There was a row. Harper was murdered and taken down to the ditch. Suddenly Watford thought of the accident idea. He went back to the tractor. By this time the tractor was pretty nearly cold and he had to switch over to petrol in order to start it again. He drove the tractor down to the ditch. It looked like an accident! It looked exactly like an accident!! But – Watford – forgot – to – switch – back – to – paraffin!!
McCRAW:	(*Stupendously overawed*) Mike! Mike, you're a genius! You're a wizard! With your brains an' my constitution … we're terrific!!!

FADE UP of music.

MYSTERY SIX

Cast:

Michael Starr . . . . Henry Oscar
Inspector McCraw . . . . Ian Sadler
Fred . . . . .Fred Yule
Bert . . . . .Dick Francis

As the opening music finishes CROSS FADE with the sound of a motor launch chug-chugging down the river. There is a background of river noises.

BERT: (*A typical cockney*) It's goin' to be a nasty night on the river, if you ask me, Sergeant. Very nasty.

FRED: Looks very much like it. Shouldn't be surprised if we don't see a bit o' fog!

BERT: 'Ope we don't. I've 'ad enough o' fog! Pull her over, Fred! Pull her over, mate!

FRED: How long 'ave you been on this job?

BERT: What? River Patrol? Very nearly six years. I started soon after … (*He stops*)

FRED: What's up?

BERT: (*Tensely*) Fred, there's some'at floating … over on the other side … it's a girl!!

BERT: (*Quickly*) Get the hook, and I'll swing across the stern so's we can …

FRED: (*Interrupting BERT: tensely*) Sergeant …

BERT: Yes?

FRED: (*A note of apprehension in his voice*) This is the third … in … three … days …

BERT: (*Grimly*) Yes. Yes, I know …

FADE SCENE on the motor launch.

FADE UP of McCRAW speaking.

McCRAW: I'll tell ye frankly, Mike, the whole business is mighty disturbing. This is the third lassie we've picked out o' the river in the last three days. (*With a sigh*) Something will have to be done, or we shall have the Home Secretary twisting our tail!

STARR: Yes, you look pretty tired, Bob!

McCRAW: I feel tired. I've been at it for nearly forty-eight hours without a break. If it wasn't for me strong constitution I'd never stand up to it.

STARR: I suppose there's no doubt in your mind that, in each particular instance, it's been simply a case of – suicide?

McCRAW: None whatever. The girls have committed suicide all right … but I'm pretty sure they each had the same motive.

STARR: (*Quietly*) What do you mean?

McCRAW: Blackmail!

STARR: Blackmail?

McCRAW: Aye, an' I'd like to get my hands on the devil who's responsible!

STARR: I had a chat to the Assistant Commissioner this morning and he mentioned a man called Dr Hartford. Is he mixed up in this business?

McCRAW: (*Thoughtfully*) Yes, but to what extent we don't exactly know … (*Confidentially*) You see, Mike, the position, so far as I see it, is simply this: the three girls we picked out o' the river refused to be blackmailed; they preferred instead to …

STARR: Commit suicide?

McCRAW: Exactly!

STARR: (*Faintly impatient*) But where does Hartford come into the picture?

McCRAW: He knew the girls. They were patients of his: fairly new patients too, I might add.

STARR: M'm …

McCRAW: Mind you, Dr Hartford isn't the only person under suspicion. There's a young fellow called Robert Staines and a woman called Dora Thomson. Ye may have heard of Dora Thomson?

STARR: Yes. She was mixed up with the Glasswell case
             about four years ago.

McCRAW: Aye, that's right.

STARR: Who was the girl Sergeant Ellison pulled out of
             the river last night?

McCRAW: A girl by the name of Betty Sanderson.
             According to the police surgeon she'd only been
             in the river about an hour and a half before they
             spotted her. We've traced her movements for the
             last two days, an' it's rather interesting, Mike.
             She had a mysterious appointment last Thursday
             – at a café in the West End, but we can't find out
             who with. If we could find out I've got a shrewd
             suspicion we'd have our man.

STARR: Or woman.

McCRAW: Aye, or woman.

STARR: What time was the appointment, do you know?

McCRAW: Between six and six forty-five.

STARR: And where was Dr Hartford exactly between six
             and six forty-five on Thursday last?

McCRAW: Now let me see … I've got the report here
             somewhere. Ah! Hartford went out to a patient
             … a Mr White of 48, Northcliffe Terrace,
             Deptford … According to Hartford's statement
             he arrived at Deptford at a quarter to six and left
             shortly after eight.

STARR: Have you verified it?

McCRAW: Aye, we verified it; but not very satisfactorily.
             You see, only two people saw the doctor: the
             nurse in charge and the patient. The nurse
             happens to be a great personal friend of Dr
             Hartford's and …

STARR: And the patient?

McCRAW: The patient died.

STARR: What about the other two people you suspect –
           Robert Staines and Dora Thomson?

McCRAW: Staines went to a party out at Camberley. He
           picked up a taxi at Paddington and arrived at
           Camberley shortly after six.

STARR: And Dora Thomson?

McCRAW: Well, she's got rather a peculiar alibi. We simply
           can't check up on it. She says she went to the
           pictures on her own an' saw Mutiny on the
           Bounty.

STARR: What time did she go into the picture house – do
           you know?

McCRAW: About half past five and she came out just after
           nine.

STARR: M'm ... when did you last see Dr Hartford, Bob?

McCRAW: Last night, an' by Jupiter I've never seen anyone
           like him. Nervous? He's like a cat on hot bricks!
           The man can hardly talk to ye for trembling.
           Frankly, Mike, it's my personal opinion that the
           laddie ...

The telephone rings and the receiver is lifted.

McCRAW: Hello? ... Yes, speaking ... (*Astonished*) What!!
           (*Quietly, after a moment*) Thank ye for ringing
           ... goodbye ...

The receiver is replaced.

STARR: What is it?

McCRAW: Dr Hartford's dead ... he shot himself ... just
           after eight o'clock this morning.

STARR: (*Slowly*) I'm not surprised.

McCRAW: (*Faintly bewildered*) What d'you mean?

STARR: It's my hunch that Dr Hartford, like the girls,
           was   being   blackmailed.   He   was   being
           blackmailed   into   throwing   suspicion   onto
           himself!!

McCRAW: (*Forcefully*) But if Hartford wasn't the blackmailer, then who was?

STARR: Don't you know, Bob?

McCRAW: Why – why of course I don't know, man! Do you?

STARR: Yes. Yes, I know, Bob …

FADE UP of music.

FADE DOWN.

ANNOUNCER: Who is the blackmailer? Do you know? Later in the programme you will hear from Michael Starr himself the solution to tonight's detective problem.

MYSTERY SIX – THE SOLUTION

ANNOUNCER: We now return you to Michael Starr for the solution to tonight's detective problem.

McCRAW: But if Hartford wasn't the blackmailer then who was?

STARR: Don't you know, Bob?

McCRAW: Why – why of course I don't know, man! Do you?

STARR: Yes. Yes, I know, Bob … (*Faintly amused*) Bob, about two weeks ago I went to a dance with Georgina. After the dance I tried to get a taxi to take her home. She lives at Camberley.

McCRAW: Camberley? Why that's where Mr Staines went – that was his alibi.

STARR: Yes, and not a very good one I'm afraid.

McCRAW: What do you mean?

STARR: You can't take a taxi to Camberley, Bob! Certainly not from Paddington! It's twenty-nine-and-a-half-miles outside of London!

McCRAW: Well, I'm jiggered!! (*Almost concerned*) But what happened to Georgina?

STARR: (*Almost a sigh of disappointment*) She has an aunt in Kensington.

FADE UP of music.

MYSTERY SEVEN
Cast:

Michael Starr . . . . Henry Oscar
Inspector McCraw . . . . Ian Sadler
Pete Kenedit . . . . Sydney Keith
Nurse Rogers . . . . Freda Falconer
A Sergeant . . . . Fred Yule

As opening music finishes FADE TO PETE KENEDIT.

PETE: (*An American commentator*) This is Pete Kenedit broadcasting to the United States of America from London, England. This week the sleepy little village of Much Drawset in the County of Barshire, finds itself – whether it likes it or not – Front Page News! Three murders in two weeks! You must admit, folks – that's pretty good going. Michael Starr, ace criminal investigator, arrived at Much Drawset in the early hours of yesterday morning – rumour has it that Chief-Inspector McCraw is feeling the effects of …

FADE PETE's voice.

FADE UP McGRAW speaking.

McCRAW: (*Relieved, yet weary*) Mike! Mike, am I glad to see ye! Am I glad to see ye!

STARR: Well, are you glad to see me, Inspector?

McGRAW: Man, ye don't know what I've been going through! Reporters! I never want to see another reporter, Mike, as long as I live!

STARR: Robert, my lad, you seem to me to be rather under the weather!

McCRAW: (*Exasperated*) Under the weather! Why, man, if it wasn't for me strong constitution I'd be under the …

STARR: (*Interrupting McCRAW*) Come on, Bob! Take a deep breath! Let's have the facts.

McCRAW: The facts! Ye won't believe a word I tell ye, Mike, it's … it's … so crazy.

STARR: Well, you can try …

McCRAW: Three people have been murdered, Mike, here … in this very village …

STARR: Yes ... Yes, I know ... it's in the newspapers. A Mr Thomas ... A Mr Briggs ... and, if I remember rightly, a Mr Calthorne.

McCRAW: Aye! (*Slowly*) But do ye know who those people were, Mike?

STARR: (*Quietly*) No?

McGRAW: They were the butcher ... the baker ... and the candlestick maker!!

STARR: (*Staggered*) What! (*Laughing*) Why, Bob, you must be crazy!

McCRAW: Man, I tell ye it's true! Thomas was the butcher, Briggs was the local baker, an' Calthorne kept a small sort o' antique shop. He specialised in making a fancy sort of candlesticks!

STARR: My golly, that's extraordinary!

McCRAW: (*Quietly: confidentially*) Mike, listen! There's somebody in this village who's crazy ... stark ... staring ... crazy ... but they're as cautious as the devil!

STARR: Have you any suspicions?

McCRAW: No. No, I don't think so.

STARR: How long have you been down here, Bob?

McCRAW: I came down after Calthorne was murdered. Before that the local people had the case in hand.

STARR: How long ago is that?

McCRAW: Just over a fortnight.

STARR: I take it, that ... nothing's happened since you've been down here?

McCRAW: No. The devil's lying low, Mike, but I've got a nasty sort o' feeling that at any minute he might suddenly ...

A door opens.

McCRAW: ... Hello, Sergeant, what is it?

SERGEANT:	(*Rather excited*) There's a Nurse Rogers downstairs, sir ... from the local hospital ... she'd like to see you, sir – it's urgent!
McCRAW:	(*Tensely*) What's happened?
SERGEANT:	Someone tried ... to ... murder ... her, sir ... about twenty minutes ago.
McCRAW:	Holy smoke!
STARR:	Come along, Inspector!

FADE SCENE.

FADE IN MICHAEL STARR speaking.

STARR:	Now take your time, Nurse. There's no hurry ... just tell us exactly what happened ...
NURSE:	(*Faint Irish accent*) Well now it's difficult to know exactly what did happen, Mr Starr. Just after five o'clock I went down to the telephone booth at the corner of Westwood Avenue. I'd got my number and was busy talking when suddenly ...
STARR:	To whom did you telephone?
NURSE:	A Dr Melford: he's a G.P. over at Northbury. I was taking down a prescription over the telephone when suddenly I heard a shot. The glass smashed, the receiver was knocked out of my hand, and ... well, that's all that happened.
STARR:	I see you've got your hand bandaged: is it badly hurt?
NURSE:	No. It was grazed slightly when the telephone was hit.
McCRAW:	(*Suspiciously*) It's your left hand I notice.
NURSE:	Yes. I was holding the telephone in my left hand.
McCRAW:	Isn't that a little unusual?

63

NURSE: (*Amused*) Not if you happen to be left-handed.

STARR laughs.

McCRAW: (*Clearing his throat with embarrassment*) M'm …

STARR: Did you, by any chance, notice anyone? When you came out of the box, I mean?

NURSE: Well … er … as a matter of fact I thought I noticed the Vicar. I'm not sure but I think he was on the other side of the road just coming out of one of the houses …

STARR: Well, in that case he'd have heard the shot, wouldn't he?

NURSE: Yes … Yes, I suppose he must have done. (*Thoughtfully*) That's odd. If he heard the shot then why didn't he come across to the box?

STARR: (*Softly*) Yes … Yes, why didn't he … I wonder?

NURSE: (*After a pause: slowly*) What – what are you looking at me like that for?

STARR: (*Quietly*) Miss Rogers, do you know what I think? (*After a moment*) I don't think there was a shot! I don't think anyone did attempt to murder you! This story of yours is just a cover-up … an attempt to convince us that you had nothing whatsoever to do with the murder of Thomas … Briggs … and Calthorne …

McCRAW: (*Suddenly – desperately*) Mike, look out!! She's got a gun!!

NURSE: Stand back! Don't move!! Don't move!! (*Suddenly she commences to laugh – wild and sinister*)

FADE UP of music.

FADE DOWN.

ANNOUNCER: What made Michael Starr suspect Nurse Rogers? Later in the programme we shall continue the adventure and you will hear from Michael Starr himself the solution to tonight's detective problem.

MYSTERY SEVEN – THE SOLUTION

ANNOUNCER: We now return you to Michael Starr for the solution to tonight's detective problem.

McCRAW: (*Suddenly – desperately*) Mike, look out!! She's got a gun!!

NURSE: Stand back! Don't move!! Don't move!! (*Suddenly she commences to laugh – wild and sinister*)

STARR: My dear Nurse Rogers, it's not a bit of use trying to exploit melodramatic ... (*Quickly*) Quick, Bob!!!

We hear the noise of a sudden scuffle.

McCRAW: I've got her! It's all right, I've ... Holy smoke, she's fainted!

STARR: Go and get the Sergeant, I'll watch her.

McCRAW: O.K. Oh – er – Mike, what the devil made ye suspect her? I – I quite swallowed that story about the telephone box.

STARR: Did you, Robert? Didn't you hear her say that she was left-handed?

McCRAW: O' course, but that's all right – she was holding the telephone in her left hand.

STARR: Exactly. But she also said she was taking down a prescription. In which case, my dear Robert, she would have been writing with her left hand and holding the telephone with her right.

McCRAW: Why – why, of course! So if her story had been true then ...

STARR: ... it would have been her right hand that was grazed by the bullet and not her left ... Exactly!

66

McCRAW: Well, I'm blowed! (*Suddenly*) Holy smoke,
             she's coming round! Watch her, Mike!
             She's pretty tough!

STARR: Don't be long, old boy. Remember ...
             (*Imitating McCRAW*) ... I haven't got your
             constitution!

FADE UP of music.

MYSTERY EIGHT
Cast:

Michael Starr . . . . Henry Oscar
Inspector McCraw . . . . Ian Sadler
Mr Tripley . . . . Dick Francis
Roland Haverford . .Preston Lockwood
Yvonne Blanchard . . . . .Rita Vale

After the opening music finishes CROSS FADE to the sound of a car travelling at about thirty or forty miles an hour.

McCRAW: Well, thank ye for a very nice dinner, Mike.

STARR: You're welcome. Where shall I drop you, Bob?

McCRAW: (*With a sigh*) Ye'd better drop me at the Yard. I've still got an awful lot to do.

STARR: At this time of the night? (*Amused*) No rest for the wicked, eh, Robert?

McCRAW: There certainly isn't. Why man, if it wasn't for me strong constitution I'd be ... (*Suddenly*) Holy smoke! Look at that girl ...

STARR: What's she going to do?

McCRAW: Why, man, she's ...

STARR: (*Quickly: desperately*) She's going to throw herself in front of the car!

McCRAW: Look out! Ye'll have to swerve, Mike! Ye'll have to swerve or ...

STARR: Hold tight! Hold tight!

There's a sudden and dramatic screeching of brakes followed by the car drawing to a standstill.

McCRAW: (*A sigh of relief*) Oooh!

STARR: Are you all right?

McCRAW: Aye ... aye, but what about yon lassie?

STARR: We missed her ... but only just ... my goodness, she was asking for it!

McCRAW: (*Grimly*) Aye, a deliberate case of attempted suicide! (*With authority*) I'd like a word with that young lady!

FADE SCENE.

FADE UP of MICHAEL STARR.

STARR: (*In an affable manner but faintly indignant*) What's the idea – dragging me along to the Yard at this time of the morning? You know perfectly well, Robert, that I make a point of never ...

McCRAW: (*Interrupting STARR*) Mike, ye remember that lassie we nearly knocked over the other night?

STARR: Why ... yes?

McCRAW: It's turned out a most interesting case.

STARR: (*Puzzled*) What do you mean?

McCRAW: I found out why the lassie attempted to commit suicide. Someone's been writing letters to her, Mike, and not exactly pleasant sort o' letters either I'm afraid.

STARR: Oh?

McCRAW: Her name is Thornton ... Mary Thornton. Apparently two or three weeks ago she started getting these scurrilous letters and ... well ... quite frankly, Mike, I think they preyed on her mind so much that the poor lassie became almost demented.

STARR: Has Miss Thornton any suspicions regarding the – er – identity of the letter writer?

McCRAW: Well – she hasn't said a great deal but I feel that she rather suspects a woman by the name of Yvonne Blanchard. Madam Blanchard lives in the same village. It's a little place called Whitetrees: about four miles this side of Bicester.

STARR: Do you suspect Madam Blanchard?

McCRAW: (*Thoughtfully*) I don't know. I don't know, Mike. As a matter of fact there are two other suspects. An actor chappie by the name of Roland Haverford and ...

STARR: Roland Haverford? He's quite a big name in the theatre world.

McCRAW:	So I believe. But judging from all accounts he's a queer sort o' bird. And then of course there's Mr Tripley.
STARR:	And who exactly is … Mr Tripley?
McCRAW:	He keeps the post office at Whitetrees. Mr Tripley is under suspicion for the simple reason that the letters were written on stationery which he obviously supplied and were posted, without exception, at his post office.
STARR:	I see. And what makes you suspect Haverford?
McCRAW:	Well, Haverford was engaged to Miss Thornton and then suddenly – and so far as we can see for no accountable reason – she broke off the engagement. Haverford was extremely bitter about it.
STARR:	M'm …
McCRAW:	(*Confidentially*) But the interesting part about this case, Mike, is this – nine years ago … in 1935 … we had identically the same sort o' case. A young girl … I think her name was Edith Bennett … received about twenty extremely scurrilous postcards. The postcards were apparently posted in Hampstead. But this is the point, Mike, an' I want you to take particular note of it! We've compared the handwriting in this case with the handwriting in the Thornton case … and it's absolutely identical!
STARR:	M'm … I'd rather like to have a word with Roland Haverford, Bob – it that possible?

McCRAW: Certainly! They're all downstairs in Superintendent Bradley's office. Roland Haverford, Mr Tripley, and Madam Blanchard. I brought them to the Yard because I want to take a handwriting test. I don't mind telling ye that they're rather indignant about it – not that it makes the slightest bit o' …

FADE VOICE.

FADE UP of several voices in conversation.
MADAM BLANCHARD is the first to be distinguished.

BLANCHARD: (*With an attractive French accent*) But why should they ask us to visit Scotland Yard? Surely they do not think that one of us wrote these disgusting letters to Miss Thornton? Why, obviously the person …

HAVERFORD: (*A clipped but extremely charming voice*) They obviously think that one of us did write the letters, Madam Blanchard, or we shouldn't be here.

TRIPLEY: (*A meek little man*) But surely they've only got to take a test of our handwriting and then they'll know who wrote the letters.

HAVERFORD: (*Pleasantly*) I wouldn't say that, Mr Tripley. After all, there's such a thing as disguising one's handwriting!

A door opens.

BLANCHARD: Yes. Yes, of course. (*Pleasantly*) Anyway, this unsavoury business has its compensations. I've always wanted to meet you, Mr Haverford. I shall never forget your performance in the Coronation Revue, Mr Cochran's Home and … Home and Beauty.

HAVERFORD: (*Amused*) I'm afraid you didn't see me in Home and Beauty, Madam! Revue isn't exactly my – er – forte!

TRIPLEY: Mr Haverford is a Shakespearean actor, Madam.

BLANCHARD: Oh, dear! Oh, dear! (*She titters, then laughs*) *HAVERFORD laughs.*

TRIPLEY: (*Quietly*) Oh, here's the Inspector.

McCRAW: I'm sorry to have kept ye all waiting, but ... Oh, this is Mr Michael Starr. With your permission I think he'd rather like to ask ye a few questions.

HAVERFORD: Certainly.

STARR: Mr Haverford, how long have you lived at Whitetrees?

HAVERFORD: Oh, er – now let me see – er – since the autumn of er ... 1936 ... Yes, 1936. Before that I was in Hampstead.

STARR: Madam Blanchard?

BLANCHARD: I came to England for the first time in July, 1938. I stayed in London for two months and then I moved out to Whitetrees. I've been there ever since.

STARR: I see. And Mr Tripley?

TRIPLEY: I was born in Whitetrees, sir. And my father before me ... we've been here for four generations.

STARR: M'm. (*Suddenly, a note of finality in his voice*) Thank you, Mr Tripley.

McCRAW: (*Surprised*) Is that all, Mike?

STARR: (*Quietly*) Yes. Yes, that's all. (*Slowly*) And I don't think the handwriting test will be necessary, do you ... Madam Blanchard?

HAVERFORD: (*Aghast*) Madam Blanchard?

BLANCHARD: What – what do you mean?

STARR: (*With authority*) I mean that you wrote those letters to Mary Thornton and the postcards to Edith Bennett! It's no good denying it, Madam Blanchard, because …

BLANCHARD: (*Defiantly*) I don't deny it! (*Quietly*) But how did you know?

FADE UP of music.

FADE DOWN.

ANNOUNCER: How did Michael Starr know that Madam Blanchard was the guilty party to tonight's detective problem?

Please turn over to see the solution to Mystery Eight.

MYSTERY EIGHT – THE SOLUTION

ANNOUNCER: We now return you to Michael Starr for the solution to tonight's detective problem.

STARR: (*With authority*) I mean that you wrote those letters to Mary Thornton and the postcards to Edith Bennett! It's no good denying it, Madam Blanchard, because ...

BLANCHARD: (*Defiantly*) I don't deny it! (*Quietly*) But how did you know?

STARR: Madam Blanchard, you said you first came to England in 1938.

BLANCHARD: Yes.

STARR: Shall I tell you why you said 1938? Because you had a suspicion that we'd already connected this case with the Bennett affair which took place in 1935.

BLANCHARD: Well?

STARR: My dear Madam Blanchard, if you only came to England for the first time in 1938, how did you manage to see the Coronation Revue? The Coronation Revue was, of course, presented during the year of the Coronation ... 1937!!

McCRAW: (*Astonished*) Well, I'm ... I'm ... I'm jiggered! I'm ... I'm stupefied! I'm – I'm ... ye know, Mike, shocks like this are not good for my constitution!

MICHAEL STARR laughs.
FADE UP of music.

MYSTERY NINE
Cast:

Michael Starr . . . . Henry Oscar

Inspector McCraw . . . . Ian Sadler

Fireman (Joe). . . . . .Dick Francis

Fireman (Bill) . . . . .Ian Sadler

Danny Mullins . . . . Fred Yule

Mrs Williams . . . . . . .Gladys Spencer

Smoky Williams . . . . . . .Dick Francis

As the opening music finishes CROSS FADE to the noise of several fire-engines and a great deal of general excitement.
At the background can be heard the raging of a fire.

BILL: (*Shouting*) Stand clear!

JOE: (*Shouting*) Stand back over there! Stand back!!

We hear the crash of falling masonry.

BILL: Blimey, this is a nice Easter Monday, I must say!

JOE: Long time since I seen a fire like this …

BRING UP the noise of the fire etc.

BILL: It's worse than the blinkin' blitz!

JOE: How's it start?

BILL: Don't ask me! He's the fellow you wants to ask – the chap with the bowler hat!

JOE: Inspector McCraw? (*Curious*) Who's the well-dressed cove?

BILL: That's Michael Starr. Cor blimey, you've 'eard of Michael Starr!

JOE: Is that him? There must be some'at up, Bill, if he's on the job!

BILL: (*Quickly*) Look out! The roof's coming down!!

FADE UP the noise of falling masonry, excited voices, general excitement and confusion.

McCRAW: Well, I've got all the details, Mike, and so far as I can make out the fire started in the basement at about six o'clock.

STARR: This business looks to me like a put-up job. I shouldn't be surprised if our old friend Smoky Williams isn't tied up with it.

McCRAW: That's mighty funny, Mike! That's exactly what I thought!

STARR: What's he doing these days?

McCRAW: Smoky? He's got a tobacconist's shop just outside Croydon. Supposed to be going straight.

About as straight as Harry Lauder's walking stick!

STARR: (*Suddenly*) Hello! Hello … look who's here!

McCRAW: (*Surprised*) Danny Mullins! Well, I'm blowed! (*Calling*) Hello, Danny!

DANNY: (*Cheery with a North Country accent*) Why, hello, Inspector! It's a champion fire you've got here!

STARR: (*Quietly*) Hello, Danny.

DANNY: (*Brightly*) Good evening, Mr Starr! An' how's your health an' temper?

STARR: Well, I shall feel much better, Danny, when I've found out who's responsible for this inferno!

DANNY: Certainly warming things up a bit, isn't it? What time did it start, Inspector?

McCRAW: Six o'clock. (*Suspiciously*) Where were you at six o'clock, Danny?

DANNY: Why, lad, you don't think I started this lot, do you? I can keep warm dodging you fellows without 'aving a blaze o' me own.

STARR: (*Amused*) Nevertheless, where were you at six o'clock, Danny?

DANNY: I was at the dentist's. (*He opens his mouth*) Take a decko!

STARR: My word! How many have you had out, Danny – six?

DANNY: (*Highly indignant*) Seven!

STARR: What did you have – gas?

DANNY: No, I didn't. I gets enough gas from my old woman without paying for it! (*Brightly*) Well, I'm off – you know where to find me if you wants me, Inspector.

McCRAW: Aye – goodbye, Danny! (*After a moment*) Are ye in a hurry, Mike?

STARR: No.

McCRAW: Come on then! Let's see if we can find Smoky Williams.

STARR: (*Laughing*) All right, Bob ...

FADE SCENE.

FADE UP of someone knocking on a door.
The door opens.

McCRAW: Is Mr Williams in?

MRS W: (*About fifty: cockney*) No, he isn't. What do you want?

McCRAW: (*With authority*) My name McCraw. Chief-Inspector McCraw of Scotland Yard.

MRS W: (*Taken aback*) Oh ... oh, well you can come in an' wait if you like.

McCRAW: Thank you. Come on, Mike.

A door opens and closes.

MRS W: ... I don't expect he'll be long! He's only slipped in next door to see to the wireless. (*Sarcastically*) Thinks he's a bit of a dab 'and at wireless does my old man! I don't think!

McCRAW and STARR laugh.

MRS W: See that thing over there. He made it 'imself. Nine valves – an' all we can get is blinkin' Forces!

STARR: (*Politely – amused*) Well, it looks very nice, Mrs Williams.

MRS W: Blimey, it ought to look nice! It used to be a chest o' drawers.

The door opens and SMOKY WILLIAMS dashes in.

SMOKY: (*Astonished*) Why ... why ... (*Pleasantly – controlling himself*) Why ... hello, guv! How are you, guv? Nice to see you, guv!

STARR: Hello, Smoky. How's the world been treating you?

SMOKY: Can't grumble, guv! Can't grumble at all! (*Suddenly*) 'Ere, come on, Ethel! Come on! Make the Inspector a cup o' tea.

STARR: (*Quietly*) Smoky …

SMOKY: Yus?

STARR: I suppose you've heard about the fire?

SMOKY: Fire? What fire?

McCRAW: In Hudson Street, laddie. A warehouse … Perkins and Brown … It started at six o'clock. (*Slowly*) Where were you at six o'clock, Smoky?

SMOKY: Me?!! Why … why I was 'ere, 'aving me tea an' listening to the news … wasn't I, Ethel?

MRS W: You was! An' grumbling about the bread … as usual!

STARR: Was anyone else here?

SMOKY: Sure – the bloke from next door an' two other fellows!

MRS W: Didn't you hear me say he was grumbling? He don't grumble when he's on his own … Oh, no! Very temperamental my husband! Must have an audience!

SMOKY: Nark it, Ethel! Nark it!

McGRAW: (*Amused*) O.K. Smoky! O.K. … Come on, Mike, let's get back to the fire. We know where to find you, Smoky.

SMOKY: Sure, guv … Sure … Come on, Ethel! Come on! Open the door for the gentlemen …

FADE SCENE.

FADE IN a street with traffic noises.

McCRAW: (*Calling*) Taxi! Taxi!

STARR: Taxi!

McCRAW:	Taxi!
STARR:	Looks pretty hopeless!
McCRAW:	Aye! Ah, it's a good job I've got a strong constitution or I'd never stand up to this racket! (*With a sigh*) This blessed case is going to be a headache, I can see that.
STARR:	(*Amused*) Do you think so, Robert?
McCRAW:	(*Arrested by STARR's tone*) Mike! Mike! Ye don't mean to say ye know who started the fire?
STARR:	Don't you, Bob?
McCRAW:	I'm blowed if I do! Was it Smoky Williams?

STARR laughs at McCRAW.

McCRAW:	Was it Danny Mullins?

STARR laughs again.

McCRAW:	(*Exasperated*) Mike! Mike! Don't laugh, man! If ye know who started the – the blankety-blank – fire … say so!

STARR continues to laugh.
FADE UP of music.

FADE DOWN.

ANNOUNCER:	Who started the fire? Do you know? Was it Smoky Williams or Danny Mullins? Later in the programme you will hear from Michael Starr himself the solution to tonight's detective problem.

MYSTERY NINE – THE SOLUTION

ANNOUNCER: We now return you to Michael Starr for the solution to tonight's detective problem.

McCRAW: Mike! Mike! Ye don't mean to say ye know who started the fire?

STARR: Don't you, Bob?

McCRAW: I'm blowed if I do! Was it Smoky Williams?

STARR laughs at McCRAW.

McCRAW: Was it Danny Mullins?

STARR laughs again.

McCRAW: (*Exasperated*) Mike! Mike! Don't laugh, man! If ye know who started the – the blankety-blank – fire … say so!

STARR continues to laugh.

STARR: (*After a moment*) My dear Inspector, it's simply a question of an alibi. Smoky Williams said that at six o'clock he was at home having his tea and listening to the six o'clock news.

McCRAW: Yes!

STARR: How could he listen to the six o'clock news on a wireless set that'll only get the Forces programme? The six o'clock news is only broadcast on the Home Service!

McCRAW: Why – why, yes, of course! Mike! Mike, you're a genius! Mike! You're a wizard!

STARR: If I was a wizard, old boy – we shouldn't be looking for a taxi! (*Suddenly: wildly excited*) Hi, taxi! Taxi!

McCRAW: Taxi!!

STARR: Taxi!!!

McCRAW: Taxi!!!!
STARR: Taxi!!!!!
FADE IN of music.

MYSTERY TEN
Cast:
Michael Starr . . . . Henry Oscar

Inspector McCraw . . . . Ian Sadler

Sergeant Brough. . . . . Fred Yule

Rev. John Hampstead . .Preston Lockwood

As the opening music finishes CROSS FADE to SERGEANT BROUGH speaking.

SERGEANT: (*With a West Country accent*) Good evening, sir.

STARR: Good evening, sergeant. My name is Michael Starr. I'm looking for an Inspector McCraw.

SERGEANT: Oh yes, sir. 'E be the gentleman 'e be that come down from Lon'on I'm thinking.

STARR: (*Amused*) Yes, sergeant.

SERGEANT: Well, 'e be 'ere a few moments ago 'e be, but 'e don't appear to be ... (*Suddenly*) Ah! 'Ere 'e be, sir!

McCRAW: (*Excitedly*) Hello, Mike. Hello. Am I glad to see ye, laddie! Did ye have a pleasant journey?

STARR: I did NOT have a pleasant journey. The train was four hours late!

McCRAW: Tut – tut ... (*Anxiously*) Tell me, Mike, did they stop the train at all outside of Rainbridge?

STARR: Yes, we were held up for about twenty minutes. (*Puzzled – faintly exasperated*) What is it, Robert? What's all the excitement about?

McCRAW: (*Slowly*) Mike, ye remember a man called Peters ... Thomas Peters? He was sentenced to fifteen years penal servitude for murdering his wife and ill-treating his three ...

STARR: (*On the word "wife"*) Yes. Yes, I remember Peters. In my opinion he was lucky to get away with fifteen years. (*After a moment*) What's happened to Peters?

McCRAW: (*After a significant pause*) He's escaped.

STARR: (*Softly – shocked*) What!!

McCRAW:	Mike, we're in a quandary! We're in a devil of a spot! I've combed the district from North to South, an' East to West, an' West to East, an' …
STARR:	(*Quickly – with an 'on the job' attitude*) When did Peters escape?
McCRAW:	Friday evening.
STARR:	That means he's been out for three days?
McCRAW:	Yes.
STARR:	You've kept a check on all roads, railway stations, airports?
McCRAW:	The whole district's surrounded, Mike! I've got a cordon from one end o' the county to the other. I won't even let the local people move without a permit!
STARR:	(*Thoughtfully*) From what I remember of Peters he's a pretty dangerous customer, isn't he, Robert?
McCRAW:	Dangerous? I should say he is dangerous, why man if he so much as … (*Suddenly – impatiently*) Yes, sergeant, what is it?
SERGEANT:	There be a gentleman 'ere, sir, called the Reverend John Hampstead. 'E be wanting a permit, sir, to visit 'is sister at …
McCRAW:	That's all right, sergeant. Give him one.
SERGEANT:	I 'ave, sir. But he'd like to have a word with you, sir.
McCRAW:	Yes, all right. Ask him in.

A pause.

HAMPSTEAD:	Ah, good evening, Inspector – I'm so sorry to trouble you.
McCRAW:	No trouble at all, sir. May I introduce Mr Michael Starr?

HAMPSTEAD: Oh, how do you do, sir? Well, Inspector, as you probably know I'm the Vicar of St Mary's at Grinford. That's the village on the other side of the river: it's about twelve miles away.

McCRAW: Yes, I know the village, sir.

HAMPSTEAD: Well, Inspector, last Saturday afternoon – I should say it would be about a quarter past four – a stranger called at the vicarage. He asked me if I would be so kind as to – er – provide him with a cup of tea. I was having tea myself so I – er – invited him into the vicarage.

STARR: What was he like – this stranger?

HAMPSTEAD: Oh … about six foot … dark … little moustache … talked rather a great deal I thought.

McCRAW: (*Rather excitedly*) By George, that sounds like Peters.

STARR: Yes.

HAMPSTEAD: He said something about trying to make his way down to Southampton. I didn't take a great deal of notice because, quite frankly, I wasn't very impressed by the fellow.

STARR: You say he talked a great deal?

HAMPSTEAD: Yes, an awful lot of nonsense about being out in Palestine and fighting with the Arabs. Obviously a pack of lies from start to finish. I'm afraid I was rather rude. I retaliated by telling him the story of Ananias.

McCRAW: Ananias?

HAMPSTEAD: (*Amused*) Really, Inspector, it's in the Bible. Ananias was the man who was struck dead for lying.

STARR:	That's right. Exodus, chapter – er – er – six.
HAMPSTEAD:	(*Highly delighted*) Oh, splendid, Mr Starr! Splendid!
McCRAW:	(*Piqued*) It's a pity you hadn't told us this before, sir!
HAMPSTEAD:	Yes, I know it's rather stupid of me, but quite frankly I never thought about this business, until I realised that I had to secure a permit in order to visit my sister.
STARR:	What was this fellow dressed like?
HAMPSTEAD:	He had a shabby sort of mackintosh on and, so far as I can remember, sir, a grey flannel jacket.
STARR:	M'm. Mr Hampstead, tell me … have you got a revolver?
HAMPSTEAD:	(*Shocked*) A revolver? Good gracious me, no sir!
STARR:	(*With authority*) Give him one, Bob!
McCRAW:	(*Surprised*) What?
STARR:	You heard what I said: give him a revolver and a pair of handcuffs.
HAMPSTEAD:	What!!
STARR:	Mr Hampstead, listen! If your story is correct and this fellow was Peters then it's my hunch that he'll return to the vicarage.
HAMPSTEAD:	But – whatever – for?
STARR:	For food! You've provided him with one meal and if he gets desperate then it's quite likely that he'll …
McCRAW:	Yes! Yes, that's pretty sound reasoning, Mike!
HAMPSTEAD:	(*Nervously*) I – I sincerely hope that he … he won't return to the vicarage! Dear me! I – I sincerely hope not!

SERGEANT:	Here's a pair of handcuffs, sir!
STARR:	Oh, thank you, sergeant. Do you know how to use them, Mr Hampstead?
HAMPSTEAD:	I'm – I'm afraid I don't, sir.
STARR:	Let me show you. Hold your hands out.

We hear a click of the handcuffs.

STARR:	That's it. There we are. They just snap together …
HAMPSTEAD:	My word, they're pretty tight. (*Amused*) Dear! Dear! I never thought I should come to this! (*A pause – faintly embarrassed*) Well … aren't you going to take them off, Mr Starr?
STARR:	(*Slowly*) No … no, not just yet, Mr … PETERS!!
SERGEANT:	Mr Peters!!
McCRAW:	What!!!!

FADE UP of music.

FADE DOWN.

ANNOUNCER:	What made Michael Starr suspect the Reverend John Hampstead? Later in the programme you will hear from Michael Starr himself the solution to tonight's detective problem.

ANNOUNCER: We now return you to Michael Starr for the solution to tonight's detective problem.

HAMPSTEAD: … Aren't you going to take them off, Mr Starr?

STARR: (*Slowly*) No. No, not just yet, Mr …. PETERS!!

SERGEANT: Mr Peters!!

McCRAW: What!!!!

STARR: (*Interrupting McCRAW*) Shall I tell you why you came here, Peters? To try and persuade the Inspector to turn all his men into the Southampton area, so that you could then …

HAMPSTEAD: That's a lie! I tell you my name is Hampstead. The Reverend John Hampstead!

STARR: Is it? Well, you don't seem very well informed, Mr Hampstead. Do you remember your reference to Ananias? Oh, yes, Ananias was the gentleman who told lies all right but you can't read about him in the book of Exodus. When I said, Exodus – chapter six – I was saying the first thing that came into my head … and yet … you agreed with me!

SERGEANT: Look out, sir!

McCRAW: Ow!

STARR: (*Quickly*) Take him away, sergeant!

SERGEANT: (*During a slight struggle*) It's all right, sir! I've got him!!

HAMPSTEAD shouts.

SERGEANT: Come along now, no rough stuff!

FADE the SERGEANT and HAMPSTEAD.

STARR: Bob, are you all right?

McCRAW: Yes. Yes, he caught me on the top of the head, but … I'm … I'm all right.

STARR: Are you sure?

McCRAW: Of course I'm sure! Why, man, with my constitution I can stand anything!

STARR: (*Quietly concerned*) You look pretty pale, old boy!

McCRAW: Nonsense! Why, I've seen the time when I could … could … Oooch! (*He swoons*)

STARR: (*Calling*) Sergeant! The Inspector's fainted! Get some water. Quick!

McCRAW: (*Disgusted*) Water!! (*Weakly*) Have ye not got any brandy?

STARR laughs.

FADE IN of music.

MYSTERY ELEVEN
Cast:

Michael Starr . . . . Henry Oscar

Inspector McCraw . . . . Ian Sadler

Geoffrey Henson . . . . Peter Cousins

Barbara Loring . . . . Molly Rankin

Yvette Courteon . . . . Rita Vale

As the opening music finishes CROSS FADE to the lifting of a telephone receiver.

A pause.

GEOFFREY: Hello ... Room service, please ... 704 ... Yes ... Hello ... Room service? This is Geoffrey Henson ... Room 704 ... I want to order dinner please ... yes, for one ... M'm – m'm – that's right ... Oh, I should say at about a quarter past eight ... Yes ... To drink? ... Well, I should rather like half a bottle of ... (*Tensely – speaking away from the phone*) What – what do you want? ... My god, put – put that gun down! (*Into the phone – tensely, terrified*) Waiter! ... Waiter, listen ... There's a girl here ... in this room ... and she's going to ...

A revolver shot is heard followed by a soft cry of fear from GEOFFREY.

Then a second revolver shot and a thud as GEOFFREY falls.

FADE SCENE.

McCRAW: Well, Mike, it's like this. The laddie was ordering dinner, he was standing by the telephone actually talking to the waiter. Suddenly, quite out of the blue, the waiter heard him say: "Waiter, listen – there's a girl here – in this room – and she's going to ..." The next thing the waiter heard was the revolver shot.

STARR: What time was that, Inspector?

McCRAW: As near as we can tell about twenty past seven.

STARR: What sort of a fellow was Geoffrey Henson?

101

McCRAW:	Oh … he seems to have been quite an amiable sort o' laddie. Perhaps a wee bit too fond of the ladies.
STARR:	M'm – I'm rather interested in this girl you were telling me about – the one he was engaged to. What's her name … Barbara …?
McCRAW:	Barbara Loring?
STARR:	Yes.
McCRAW:	She's a queer sort o' lassie: rather temperamental I should imagine.
STARR:	When was the last time she saw Henson, do you know?
McCRAW:	Well, according to what she says, Mike, over three weeks ago.
STARR:	She didn't see him last night then?
McCRAW:	No … no, apparently not.
STARR:	(*Curious*) Bob, what made Henson decide to have dinner in his room … alone … was that a usual procedure?
McCRAW:	M'm – it wasn't unusual for him – especially on a Sunday.
STARR:	I see.
McCRAW:	This gal, Mike, Barbara Loring, she's wasn't the only lassie he'd been engaged to, ye know. He was engaged to a French gal for a short time, a Mademoiselle Courteon.
STARR:	Is Mademoiselle Courteon still over here?
McCRAW:	Oh, good gracious me, yes. She's lived in this country for years. As a matter of fact I've got an appointment to see her at two o'clock.
STARR:	Two o'clock? O.K., I'll try and make it.
McCRAW:	I wish you would, Mike.
STARR:	I'd rather like to have a word with that other girl too, Bob. Barbara … Loring …

McCRAW:	I tried to get hold of Miss Loring this morning but she was out. I've left a message for her.
STARR:	Have you any idea how she spent last night?
McCRAW:	Aye ... she went to a theatre.
STARR:	What – on a Sunday?
McCRAW:	It was a charity show, Mike – at The Grand.
STARR:	I see. (*Suddenly*) What time is it now?
McCRAW:	Twelve fifteen.
STARR:	Good heavens, and I'd a date at twelve o'clock! (*Quickly*) I'll be back by two, Robert.
McCRAW:	O.K. laddie! O.K.!

FADE SCENE.

FADE UP of MICHAEL STARR.

STARR:	... and you say, Miss Loring, that the last time you saw Mr Henson was just over three weeks ago.
BARBARA:	Three weeks last Thursday to be precise, Mr Starr.
STARR:	M'm. I'm given to understand that you went to the theatre last night – a charity show at The Grand – is that correct?
BARBARA:	Yes.
STARR:	Who was on the programme, Miss Loring – can you remember?
BARBARA:	Why, of course I can remember! The show started with a dance orchestra, then there was a singer – I think her name was Adele Forsythe – then there was a little comedian fellow, you know that awfully funny little man who always dresses up as a bus conductress ... (*Amused*) ... quite the funniest make-up I've ever seen!

103

McCRAW:	Bobby Maker …
BARBARA:	That's right, Inspector – Bobby Maker. Then there was a dramatic sketch, then the dance orchestra, and as a sort of finale we had community singing. (*With gentle sarcasm*) Is that correct, Mr Starr? I see you've got the programme in front of you.
STARR:	(*Amused*) Yes, that's quite correct, Miss Loring. Thank you. (*After a moment*) And now, mademoiselle, if you would be so …
YVETTE:	(*Interrupting STARR – annoyed*) It's not a bit of use asking me where I spent last night because … I haven't the slightest intention of telling you!
McCRAW:	(*Annoyed*) I'm afraid ye've got to tell us, missie, because if ye don't then we shall assume …
STARR:	(*Gently – interrupting McCRAW*) Please understand, mademoiselle, we don't wish to pry into your private affairs – er – unnecessarily. But this, to say the least, is rather serious. Mr Henson was murdered last night at approximately twenty past seven. (*Slowly – with charm*) Where were you last night, mademoiselle, at twenty minutes past seven?
YVETTE:	I – I was with a friend … out at Richmond … a gentleman friend, you understand.
STARR:	What time did you go out there?
YVETTE:	During the afternoon – about three o'clock …
STARR:	And you left?
YVETTE:	It – it was very late when I left.
STARR:	After seven twenty?
YVETTE:	Considerably after seven twenty, monsieur.

STARR:	I see. When was the first time you heard about ... Mr Henson?
YVETTE:	Why, when I saw the newspapers ... of course. It – it was a dreadful shock.
STARR:	M'm. (*Suddenly*) Inspector, can we go into the Superintendent's office for a moment?
McCRAW:	(*Surprised*) Why, yes, of course. This way, Mike!

A door opens and closes.
A slight pause.

McCRAW:	(*Tensely*) What is it, Mike?
STARR:	(*Seriously*) I want you to get a warrant out, Bob.
McCRAW:	A warrant!
STARR:	Yes. For the woman who murdered Geoffrey Henson.
McCRAW:	(*Astounded*) You mean to say ... you know who murdered her?
STARR:	Yes. Yes, I know, Inspector. And you'd better get rid of ...

FADE STARR's voice.
FADE UP music.
FADE DOWN.

ANNOUNCER:	Who murdered Geoffrey Henson? Was it Barbara Loring or Mademoiselle Courteon? Later in the programme you will hear from Michael Starr himself the solution to tonight's detective problem.

ANNOUNCER: We now return to Michael Starr for the solution to tonight's detective problem.

McCRAW: A warrant!

STARR: Yes. For the woman who murdered Geoffrey Henson.

McCRAW: (*Astounded*) You mean to say … you know who murdered her?

STARR: Yes. Yes, I know, Inspector. And you'd better get rid of Mademoiselle Courteon.

McCRAW: You mean …?

STARR: I mean that Barbara Loring murdered Geoffrey Henson. That alibi of hers was a phoney. She never went to that charity concert.

McCRAW: But man she knew every single item on the programme!

STARR: Of course she did, for the simple reason that she took the trouble to check up on it. But she made a mistake, Robert, my lad!

McCRAW: What do you mean?

STARR: That comedian fellow she talked about – Bobby Maker – he never dressed himself up as a bus conductress.

McCRAW: Why, don't be silly, Mike, he always dresses himself up as a bus conductress. That's his act!

STARR: Not on a Sunday, old boy. Don't forget the L.C.C.! No costumes!! No make-up!!

McCRAW: Well, I'm blowed! Well, I'm … Mike! Mike, why man, with …

STARR: (*Imitating McCRAW*) With your constitution
              an' my brains we're terrific!
STARR and McCRAW roar with laughter.
FADE IN of music.

MYSTERY TWELVE

Cast:

As the opening music finishes CROSS FADE to a telephone ringing and the receiver being lifted.

STARR: Hello – this is Michael Starr speaking.

McCRAW: (*Anxiously*) Is that you, Mike?

STARR: Oh, hello, Robert. What's the trouble?

McCRAW: Mike, I'm in a quandary. I've got a real ticklish situation on hand. In fact, if it wasn't for me strong constitution, I'd probably be having a …

STARR: (*On the word 'constitution'*) Yes, well you can count me out old boy. (*Determined*) I've got a date with Georgina and nothing on earth is going to make me cancel it.

McCRAW: Nothin'?

STARR: Absolutely nothing!

McCRAW: (*Softly – urgent*) It's serious, Mike!

STARR: I don't care if they've murdered the Assistant Commissioner!

McCRAW: O.K. O.K., if that's final.

STARR: That's final!

McCRAW: (*With a sigh*) Well … goodbye laddie.

STARR: (*Reluctantly*) What's it all about anyway?

McCRAW: Oh … a lassie.

STARR: What sort of a lassie?

McCRAW: (*Suddenly*) Mike, she's got the face of Hedy Lamarr, the voice of Marlene Dietrich, the figure of Rosalind Russell, and the legs of Claudette Colbert!

STARR: (*Immediately on the job*) Good heavens, old boy – this sounds frightfully serious!

McCRAW: It is, Mike, devilishly serious!

STARR: Well, why the Dickens didn't you say so? I'll be round in fifteen minutes …

111

FADE SCENE.

FADE IN McCRAW speaking.

McCRAW: Mike, I owe ye an apology but if it's any consolation to ye ...

STARR: Never mind the apologies, old boy! Where's this girl you were telling me about? The one with the Hollywood personality!

McCRAW: That's just the point, Mike. There – er – there isn't a girl. As a matter of fact, there isn't a lassie in the case at all.

STARR: (*Pretending to be furious*) Why you double-crossing son of a haggis. I've a good mind to ...

McCRAW: Mike! Mike, control yourself!

STARR: (*Sharply*) Come on then! What is it? What's it all about?

McCRAW: Mike, I want ye to listen very carefully. Yesterday morning a certain Mr Castleford was visited by his doctor. The doctor told Castleford that he would make up a bottle of medicine for him and a box of special ointment. Castleford was instructed to call round to the doctor's surgery and pick up the medicine and ointment any time after six o'clock in the evening. At about half past seven last night Castleford went round to the surgery. He walked in through the front door and took the medicine and the box of ointment off the usual sort of shelf just inside the waiting room. When he got home Mr Castleford had a little supper and then he ... (*Slowly*) ... he took a dose of the medicine.

STARR: Well?

112

McCRAW:	He died ... he died, Mike! He died from arsenic poisoning!
STARR:	(*Softly*) Good heavens!
McCRAW:	Someone had walked into the waiting room prior to the arrival of Mr Castleford and had calmly inserted arsenic into the bottle of medicine. Now this is the interesting point, Mike. A young fellow called Denis Sheriden visited the waiting room at about a quarter to seven in order to pick up a bottle of medicine and some ointment. He admits that the room was empty and that he had ample opportunity of inserting the arsenic.
STARR:	But had he a motive?
McCRAW:	Had he a motive! Three years ago the laddie was sent to prison for six months on evidence supplied, mark you, by Mr Castleford! Yes, frankly Mike, without being prejudiced, I don't like young Sheriden – but I'm not at all sure that he's guilty.
STARR:	I take it that he pleads not guilty?
McCRAW:	Pleads is hardly the right word! He emphatically insists that he's not guilty. He even goes so far as to say that he wasn't aware of the fact that Mr Castleford was a patient of Dr Smith's.
STARR:	M'm – I'd like a word with Sheriden. Where is he – downstairs?
McCRAW:	Yes. In the Superintendent's office.
STARR:	Let's go down ...

FADE SCENE.

FADE IN STARR speaking.

STARR:	What time was it when you visited the surgery, Mr Sheriden?
SHERIDEN:	(*Rather impetuously*) I've already told you – it was about a quarter to seven.
STARR:	And how many bottles of medicine were there on the shelf – can you remember?
SHERIDEN:	I should say about half-a-dozen … and two boxes of ointment, neither of which were for Mr Castleford.
STARR:	How do you know?
SHERIDEN:	Because one box was for me and the other was for a Miss Forsythe – I distinctly remember the name.
McCRAW:	But listen, laddie – the nurse says that Mr Castleford's medicine was put on the shelf at five minutes to six. Therefore, it must have been there at a quarter to seven.
SHERIDEN:	(*Emphatically: almost losing his temper*) Well, I'm sorry to disappoint you, Inspector, but I can assure you that Mr Castleford's medicine was not on the shelf at a quarter to seven!
STARR:	Did you know that Mr Castleford was a patient of Dr Smith's?
SHERIDEN:	No! And I've still only got the Inspector's word for it!
McCRAW:	(*Angrily*) What d'you mean?
SHERIDEN:	(*Forcefully annoyed*) You've told me that Castleford picked up a bottle of medicine and one hour later died from arsenic poisoning! That's all you've told me!
McCRAW:	(*Shouting back at SHERIDEN*) Well?

SHERIDEN: Well, how do I know that the arsenic was in the medicine! For all I know you might just be trying to – to pin something on me!

McCRAW: I can assure you that we're not, Mr Sheriden!

SHERIDEN: Then what's the point of all these silly questions?

STARR: (*Very politely*) The point is, Mr Sheriden, that by asking you a lot of – er – comparatively stupid questions you might – er – make a slip.

SHERIDEN: (*With sarcasm*) Yes, well, since I had nothing whatever to do with the affair it isn't very likely that I shall make – what you choose to call a slip, is it, Mr Starr?

A pause.

SHERIDEN: Why are you smiling?

STARR: (*Politely*) I'm smiling, Mr Sheriden, because you see ... you've already made one!

FADE UP of music.
FADE DOWN.

ANNOUNCER: Why does Michael Starr suspect Denis Sheriden? Later in the programme you will hear from Michael Starr himself the solution to tonight's detective problem.

MYSTERY TWELVE – THE SOLUTION

ANNOUNCER: We now return you to Michael Starr for the solution to tonight's detective problem.

SHERIDEN: (*With sarcasm*) Yes, well, since I had nothing whatever to do with the affair it isn't very likely that I shall make – what you choose to call a slip, is it, Mr Starr?

A pause.

SHERIDEN: Why are you smiling?

STARR: (*Politely*) I'm smiling, Mr Sheriden, because you see ... you've already made one!

SHERIDEN: (*Angrily*) What do you mean?

STARR: The Inspector told you that Mr Castleford picked up a bottle of medicine and one hour later died from arsenic poisoning – that's all he told you!

SHERIDEN: Yes!

STARR: Then – how did you know that Mr Castleford was expecting a box of ointment?!!

McCRAW: (*Suddenly*) Look out Mike!

STARR: Ow!

McCRAW: Whoo, what a wallop! Take that laddie!

SHERIDEN falls with a crash.

McCRAW: Mike! Mike! Are you all right?

STARR: (*Dazed*) I say, what – what a wallop! Just – just look at my eye! (*Indignantly amused*) Bob, this is all wrong! I'm – I'm the detective! People like me don't get black eyes!

McCRAW: (*Highly amused*) You wait till tomorrow, laddie!

STARR laughs.
FADE IN of music.

MYSTERY THIRTEEN

Cast:

Michael Starr . . . . Henry Oscar
Inspector McCraw . . . . Ian Sadler
Dr Armstrong . . . . Cyril Gardiner
Professor Melford . . . . Arthur Ridley

As the opening music finishes CROSS FADE to the sound of a motor car. The car slows down and eventually stops. The car door opens and closes.

MICHAEL STARR is heard whistling – the whistle is obviously a signal.

McCRAW: (*A tense whisper*) Is that you, Mike?

STARR: (*From the background*) Yes … Where the devil are you?

McCRAW: I'm over here, laddie, near the gate!

STARR: (*Impatiently – a little nearer*) I can't see you, Bob.

McCRAW: Over here, laddie.

STARR and McCRAW meet.

STARR: My word, it's a foul night! I had a Dickens of a job finding this place.

McCRAW: Aye, I expect you did.

STARR: (*Faintly surprised*) Is this Kenvick Manor? I always imagined a rather …

McCRAW: No. No … this is just the lodge, Mike. The house is about a quarter of a mile up the drive.

STARR: Oh, yes. Pretty grim looking place too from what I can see of it.

McCRAW: Aye, it's not exactly my idea of a health resort. (*Brightening up*) How are ye, Mike – fine?

STARR: (*Imitating MCCRAW's accent*) No! I have na' got your constitution an' I don't like getting out o' bed at three o' clock in the morning.

McCRAW: (*After a laugh*) I'm sorry, Mike, but I'm in rather a quandary and … Oh, well, come on, laddie! Let's go up to the house!

STARR: No, no! Just a minute! Don't be in such a hurry! (*Slowly*) What's it all about, Bob?

121

McCRAW:	Well, Mike, as ye probably know this place – Kenvick Manor – belongs to a Professor Melford. He was, I believe, Professor of English at Columbia University, but … oh, that's goin' back ten or fifteen years. The Professor's a queer sort o' cove, Mike, almost I suppose what ye might call a recluse. Well, about ten o'clock this evening I was driving past this place when suddenly a man dashed out o' the drive. Fortunately me brakes were pretty good or otherwise I'm afraid …
STARR:	Was it the Professor?
McCRAW:	Aye! And he certainly was in a devil of a state! Apparently his valet and general factotum, a chappie by the name of Hollins, had committed suicide. We went back to the house and I had a look at the old boy. He was dead all right – an' he wasn't a pretty sight, Mike.
STARR:	Go on.
McCRAW:	I sent down to the local station for the police surgeon. A chappie by the name of Armstrong. He examined Hollins and expressed the opinion that he'd been dead about half an hour. He also expressed the opinion, Mike, that it wasn't suicide.
STARR:	I see. Well, supposing for a moment that we accept the theory that Hollins was murdered by the Professor. What would you suggest as a possible motive?
McCRAW:	I can't suggest anything, Mike. The Professor was devoted to the laddie. Absolutely devoted!
STARR:	M'm. Is the doctor still at the house?

122

McCRAW:	Yes. Yes, of course.
STARR:	Then come on, Bob. I'd like a word with him.
McCRAW:	Ye'll find Dr Armstrong very reliable, Mike. He was attached to the Yard at one time but …

FADE SCENE.

FADE UP DR ARMSTRONG.

DOCTOR:	Well, you can see the bullet wound for yourself, Mr Starr. Do you think it was suicide?
STARR:	M'm.
McCRAW:	It could na' have been suicide.
MELFORD:	But – but if it wasn't suicide what – what happened? Surely you don't think he … he … was murdered?
McCRAW:	I'm afraid that's the only alternative, Professor.
STARR:	When was the last time you saw Hollins … alive?
MELFORD:	It would be about eight o'clock. I was upstairs in the study. He brought me a cup of coffee and a book I'd been looking for.
McCRAW:	There was a book on the floor near the body … Oh, here it is!
STARR:	Charles Lamb … "Essays of Elia" … is this the book, Professor?
MELFORD:	No. No, this was a novel. Blackmore's "Lavengro". As a matter of fact I thought I'd lost the copy.
STARR:	That was at eight o'clock, you say?
MELFORD:	Yes. As near as I can remember – eight o'clock.
STARR:	Did he seem perfectly normal? I mean he …

MELFORD: Perfectly.

STARR: How was he dressed?

MELFORD: (*Surprised by the question*) How – how was he dressed? Why … just the same as he is now of course. Not very well dressed, I'm afraid. Poor Hollins!

DOCTOR: How old would you say he was, Professor?

MELFORD: Hollins? He was two years older than I am, doctor. Which made him sixty-three. It's funny you should ask that because I was only chaffing the poor fellow about …

In the background a telephone is ringing.

MELFORD: … his age last night when he … hello! Is that the telephone?

McCRAW: Aye!

MELFORD: Excuse me, gentlemen. It's in the library.

A pause.

A door opens and closes.

McCRAW: Well, what do you make of things, Mike?

DOCTOR: An interesting case, don't you think so, Mr Starr?

STARR: Yes. Yes, most interesting.

MccRAW: Well, Mike. Was Hollins murdered?

STARR: No.

DOCTOR: No?!!

McCRAW: You mean – it was suicide after all?

STARR: No, Inspector … it wasn't suicide.

McCRAW: (*Bewildered*) It – it wasn't suicide!

STARR: No, Inspector … it wasn't suicide!

DOCTOR: You mean it … it was an accident?

STARR: No, doctor – it wasn't an accident!

McCRAW: Holy smoke!! You mean to say Hollins didn't commit suicide! He wasn't murdered!! And – and it wasn't an accident!!

STARR:	That's right, Bob!
McCRAW:	Why ... Mike ... I – I – I (*A deep breath*) Laddie, I'm ... speechless ...

FADE UP of music.
FADE DOWN.

ANNOUNCER:	What is the mystery of Kenvick Manor? Do you know? Later in the programme you will hear from Michael Starr himself the solution to tonight's detective problem.

MYSTERY THIRTEEN – THE SOLUTION

ANNOUNCER: We now return you to Michael Starr for the solution to tonight's detective problem.

McCRAW: Holy smoke!! You mean to say Hollins didn't commit suicide! He wasn't murdered!! And – and it wasn't an accident!!

STARR: That's right, Bob!

McCRAW: Why ... Mike ... I – I – I (*A deep breath*) Laddie, I'm ... speechless ...

STARR: My dear Bob, it's really quite simple when you come to think about it. You see ... Hollins isn't dead ...

McCRAW: Hollins – isn't dead!!

DOCTOR: Hollins isn't ... Then who the devil is this fellow?

STARR: Professor Melford.

DOCTOR: What!!

McCRAW: Mike!! Mike, man, have ye taken leave of your senses?

STARR: (*Briskly*) Listen! When you drove past the gate tonight Hollins, the valet, was making a getaway. When you stopped him, he became frightened, told you he was Professor Melford, and brought you back to the house.

McCRAW: Ye mean to say the fellow we've been talking to is really the valet and this chappie here is the Professor?

STARR: Exactly! Look at the dead man – look at the suit he's wearing.

McCRAW: It's the sort o' suit a servant would wear!

STARR:	Of course it is – it belongs to Hollins – but it's too small for this fellow. Look at the book you found by the body, Robert. "Essays of Elia" by Charles Lamb. Would a valet read the "Essays of Elia"?
DOCTOR:	He might.
STARR:	Yes, but there's one other point, doctor. Our friend, the so-called Professor, said that at eight o'clock Hollins took him a cup of coffee and a copy of a book he'd been looking for. A novel – Blackmore's "Lavengro".
DOCTOR:	Well?
McCRAW:	What about "Lavengro"?
STARR:	Only that it happens to have been written by George Borrow, Bob. Blackmore's "Lavengro"! (*With a laugh*) What an extraordinary statement for a Professor of English!

FADE IN of music.

MYSTERY FOURTEEN
Cast:

Michael Starr . . . . Henry Oscar

Inspector McCraw . . . . Ian Sadler

Mr Carson . . . . Cyril Gardiner

Mona Van Elson . . . . Rita Vale

As the opening music finishes CROSS FADE to Mr CARSON who is very suave and sure of himself. He is talking to MONA VAN ELSON who is intensely angry and rather frightened.

CARSON: (*Quietly*) Is that your last word?

MONA: Yes. Yes, that's my last word!

CARSON: Well, I do sincerely hope that you are not labouring under the impression that I'm bluffing, Mrs Van Elson, because I can assure you that I'm not.

MONA: I don't care whether you're bluffing or not! I'm not going to pay you six hundred pounds! Why – why this is blackmail!

CARSON: (*Laughing*) Of course it's blackmail! I make no bones about it! And as a professional blackmailer, Mrs Van Elson, I assure you that the letters are extremely cheap at six hundred pounds!

MONA: It isn't the six hundred pounds, it's …

CARSON: (*Amused*) Oh dear! I know exactly what you're going to say! It's the principle of the thing! Why do people always say it's the principle of the thing?

MONA: (*Very angrily*) Get out! You heard what I said – get out!

CARSON: My dear Mrs Van Elson, if I leave this room these letters – these extremely sentimental school girlish letters – will be sent direct to the editor of The Daily Reflector. You know what that means! It means publicity! A great deal of unpleasant publicity.

MONA: I'm not afraid of publicity!

CARSON: (*Amused*) Aren't you? Then why don't you get in touch with Scotland Yard?

MONA: (*Grimly*) Mr Carson – I think that's a very
             good idea! And if you think I'm only …

FADE SCENE.

FADE IN McCRAW speaking.

McCRAW: Mike, ye've got to hand it to the woman!
             She's made herself the laughing stock of the
             whole country – but she's stuck to her guns!

STARR: Yes, but what happened about this fellow
             Carson? Have you arrested him?

McCRAW: Of course we haven't arrested him! How the
             devil can we? Don't ye understand what
             happened, Mike? Just over a week ago, on the
             sixth to be precise, this fellow Carson paid
             Mrs Van Elson a visit, he demanded six
             hundred pounds in return for certain
             unfortunate letters which the lady had written.
             Now the point is this, Mike. Carson denies
             having visited Mrs Van Elson and we simply
             can't prove that he did!

STARR: M'm. What time was the interview supposed
             to have taken place?

McCRAW: In the afternoon. According to Mrs Van Elson
             Carson arrived just before a quarter to two and
             left about half past.

STARR: Didn't any of the servants see him?

McCRAW: No. Unfortunately no one saw him.

STARR: M'm – what's Carson's side of the story?

McCRAW: It's pretty straight forward. He says he never
             left his flat in Curzon Street and spent the best
             part of the afternoon telephoning.

STARR: Have you checked up on this?

McCRAW: Aye. Apparently at about a quarter to two he
             telephoned his stockbroker – a chappie by the

132

name of Hudson – and gave instructions about some shares he wanted to dispose of. Carson says they talked for about twenty minutes and then Hudson got in touch with the Stock Exchange and sold the shares. He rang Carson back at about a quarter past two and this conversation lasted until about ... oh ... almost ten to three.

STARR: So, in other words, from approximately a quarter to two until a quarter to three Carson was on the telephone talking to his stockbroker?

McCRAW: Aye! Except of course for the brief interlude between the calls whilst ...

STARR: Hudson got in touch with the Stock Exchange ...

McCRAW: Aye!

STARR: Does Hudson confirm the telephone conversations?

McCRAW: Emphatically! I tell ye, Mike, this case has got me rattled! We know Carson's guilty but there doesn't seem to be the slightest chance o' proving it! If it wasn't for me strong constitution I don't really think I'd be ...

STARR: Never mind your constitution, Robert! Now listen! What sort of a fellow is this stockbroker?

McCRAW: Oh, quite a decent sort ... youngish ...

STARR: I suppose it's occurred to you that ...

McCRAW: That Carson might be blackmailing the stockbroker into providing him with an alibi?

STARR: Yes.

McCRAW: Aye, that did occur to me. But how the devil are we going to prove it? In fact, we can't

	prove it, Mike, unless Carson's made a slip and so far as I ...
STARR:	That's just the point, Bob. Carson has made a slip.
McCRAW:	WHAT!
STARR:	(*Rather amused*) You know, Robert, this is really quite a simple case when you start to think about it ... (*He chuckles*)

FADE IN of music.
FADE DOWN.

| ANNOUNCER: | Later in the programme you will hear from Michael Starr himself the solution to tonight's detective problem. |

Please turn over for the solution to mystery fourteen.

ANNOUNCER: We now return you to Michael Starr for the solution to tonight's detective problem.

STARR: That's just the point, Bob. Carson has made a slip.

McCRAW: WHAT?

STARR: (*Rather amused*) You know, Robert, this is really quite a simple case when you start to think about it … (*He chuckles*)

McCRAW: Mike. Mike, what do you mean?

STARR: Robert, my lad. Listen! On the sixth of May at a quarter to two Carson telephoned his stockbroker. Correct?

McCRAW: Correct.

STARR: They talked for approximately twenty minutes, during the course of which conversation Carson instructed his broker to sell certain shares. This conversation terminated at roughly about five minutes past two. Correct?

McCRAW: Correct.

STARR: Ten minutes later at a quarter past two Hudson telephoned through to Carson with the news that he'd been in touch with the Stock Exchange and sold the shares. This conversation lasted until about … oh … a quarter to three. Correct?

McCRAW: Correct.

STARR: And that's Mr Carson's alibi.

McCRAW: Aye! And it's just about as water tight as anything can be.

STARR:	Water tight my … umbrella! I've never heard such poppycock in all my life! Think, Robert, my lad! Think! All this is supposed to have happened on the sixth of May! The sixth of May! A Saturday! How the devil could Hudson get in touch with the Stock Exchange on a Saturday afternoon!
McCRAW:	Well, I'm … I'm … (*Weakly*) Mike … Mike, I think I could do with a brandy.
STARR:	You'll have a pink gin … and like it!

FADE IN of music.

MYSTERY FIFTEEN
Cast:

Michael Starr . . . . Henry Oscar
Inspector McCraw . . . . Ian Sadler
Denis . . . . .Fred Yule
Rodgers . . . . .Preston Lockwood

As the opening music finishes CROSS FADE to the sound of a motor car standing still ticking-over.

RODGERS: (*Nervously*) Are ... you ... feeling ... o.k.?
DENIS: Sure.
RODGERS: You ... know ... what ... to ... do?
DENIS: Leave it to me, Johnny!
RODGERS: Now don't forget ... drive straight up to the shop window and as soon as ...
DENIS: (*With a nervous little laugh*) Smash ... and ... grab ... isn't exactly my line of country ...
DENIS: You'll be all right. (*Seriously*) Now don't smash the window until you hear me rev the car.
RODGERS: O.K.
DENIS: Come on, let's get going.

The car moves away and gathers speed.
FADE OUT.

FADE In the car. With a grinding of brakes the car draws to a standstill. The noise of the car engine increases and simultaneously is heard the smashing of a shop window.
FADE UP excited voices and police whistles.

DENIS: (*Tensely*) Have you got the necklace?
RODGERS: (*Breathlessly*) Yes.
DENIS: (*Quickly*) Then jump in ...
RODGERS: Hadn't we better ...
DENIS: (*Tensely: quickly*) Jump to it!!

The car door slams and the car races away.
FADE SCENE on the car and background noises.

FADE IN McCRAW speaking.

McCRAW: Well, I've sent for ye before we're actually in trouble, Mike. But I can smell it – so there's

	no point in waiting till the last minute. As my old father used to say, if ye haven't got the brains yeself laddie, pick somebody else's.
STARR:	He seems to have been a pretty shrewd old bird – your father!
McCRAW:	Aye – and he'd a grand constitution! Why man, I've seen the day when …
STARR:	(*Gently interrupting McCRAW*) Bob … what's it all about?
McCRAW:	What? Oh, yes. Aye … well, yesterday afternoon, Mike, at about half past four a jewellers shop on the outskirts of Bexley was raided … the shop window smashed to pieces and a necklace was stolen … a diamond necklace valued at about two or three thousand pounds.
STARR:	This is interesting. It's not in the newspapers.
McCRAW:	No, we've kept it out o' the papers. It's a pretty high class firm – Smith and Carpenter – and they're not at all keen on the publicity.
STARR:	I see. Do you suspect anyone?
McCRAW:	Aye, as a matter of fact we do, Mike. Two fellows by the name of Rodgers and Denis. I've had a word with 'em, Mike, but so far as I can gather they've both got perfect alibis.
STARR:	What do you call a perfect alibi, Bob?
McCRAW:	Well, apparently they both spent the day at Leamington Spa. Rodgers has a sister at Leamington. They left Euston on the 9.10 and came back on the 6.32.
STARR:	You've checked this, I suppose, with the sister?
McCRAW:	Oh, aye – she confirms it all right.

STARR:	(*Thoughtfully*) I remember Denis. He was mixed up with the Salisbury case about three or four years ago. Untrustworthy sort of blighter. I'd like a word with him, Bob.
McCRAW:	By all means, laddie. They're both in the Superintendent's office. Denis is just a little too cocksure for my liking but the other fellow ...

FADE SCENE.

FADE UP DENIS talking.

DENIS:	My dear Superintendent ...
McCRAW:	Inspector, if ye don't mind ...
DENIS:	My dear Inspector, we've already told you that we spent the day in Leamington. We left Euston on the ...
STARR:	(*Interrupting DENIS – quite pleasantly*) Mr Denis, tell me, have you ever been to Bexley?
DENIS:	Why – why yes. I think so.
STARR:	Have you, Mr – er – Rodgers?
RODGERS:	Why, yes – but it must be two or three years ago.
STARR:	I see. (*After a moment*) The Inspector's already told you about the robbery, can you – er – recall to mind the jewellers in question?
DENIS:	What did they call the firm?
STARR:	Smith and Carpenter.
DENIS:	Oh, yes.
RODGERS:	They're in Queen Street, aren't they?
McCRAW:	No, Mr Rogers, they're on the main Bexley Road.
RODGERS:	(*Amused*) Sorry.
STARR:	Do you still run a car, Mr Denis?
DENIS:	Yes. A small grey 10 HRP. DCX 294.

STARR:	Did anyone see the car at Bexley?
McCRAW:	Aye, it was a blue saloon. MJC 856.
RODGERS:	(*Laughing*) You don't seem to be having any luck, do you, Mr Starr?
STARR:	(*Quietly*) That's rather a matter of opinion.
RODGERS:	(*No longer amused*) What do you mean?
STARR:	I mean that your alibi is phoney. Just about as phoney as ...
DENIS:	(*Suddenly – dramatically*) Stand back!
McCRAW:	Put that gun down man or ...
DENIS:	Stand back – and keep your mouth shut! Lock the door, Johnny!
RODGERS:	(*Tensely*) O.K.
DENIS:	Now, Mr Starr, before I shoot the grin off that face of yours ... What made you suspicious?

FADE UP of music.

FADE DOWN.

ANNOUNCER:	What made Michael Starr suspect Denis and Rodgers? Do you know? Later in the programme you will hear from Michael Starr himself the solution to tonight's detective problem.

Please turn over for the solution to mystery fifteen.

MYSTERY FIFTEEN – THE SOLUTION

ANNOUNCER: We now return you to Michael Starr for the solution to tonight's detective problem.

DENIS: Stand back – and keep your mouth shut! Lock the door, Johnny!

RODGERS: (*Tensely*) O.K.

DENIS: Now, Mr Starr, before I shoot the grin off that face of yours ... What made you suspicious?

STARR: Shall I tell you what made me suspicious, Mr Denis? Well, in the first place ... (*Suddenly*) Quickly, Bob!

A loud crash is heard and a cry of pain from Denis.

McCRAW: Take that, laddie!

A second crash is heard.

STARR: (*Breathlessly*) Are you all right, Bob?

McCRAW: Aye! Aye, I'm o.k. Phew!

STARR laughs.

McCRAW: Mike! Mike, what made ye suspicious?

STARR: Well, I was just about to put the blighters through a pretty stiff cross-examination when I suddenly realised what a terrible mistake they'd made.

McCRAW: But what was it?

STARR: (*Laughing*) Mr dear Robert, you can't go to Leamington from Euston. It's G.W.R.!!

McCRAW: Well ... they certainly made an L.M.S. of things!

STARR: Ooooh, what raillery!

STARR and McGRAW both laugh.

FADE UP of music.

MYSTERY SIXTEEN
Cast:

Michael Starr . . . . Henry Oscar

Inspector McCraw . . . . Ian Sadler

Gerard Lester . . . . Dick Francis

Pitman . . . . .Basil Jones

As the opening music finishes CROSS FADE to the dialling of a telephone.

LESTER: (*Rather excited and nervous*) Hello? Hello? Is
               that – White – Whitehall – 1- 2 – 1 – 2? This is
               Gerard Lester speaking ... I'm the Secretary of
               the Medusa Club ... Yes, the Medusa Club ...
               49a Pall Mall ... Could you send someone
               round straight away, I mean ... (*Flustered*)
               What? ... Well ... it's ... it's about Lord
               Harringson ... Yes, Lord Harringson ... He's –
               he's dead! ... Well, I'm afraid I couldn't say
               because you see the ...

FADE SCENE.

FADE IN McCRAW.

McCRAW: Mike! Mike, I'm in a quandary! If it wasn't for
               me strong ...

STARR: (*On the word 'quandary'*) What again?

STARR laughs.

McCRAW: Aye, it's all right laughing, laddie! But this is
               serious! Devilishly serious!

STARR: I suppose it's the Harringson case?

McCRAW: Aye! (*Irritated*) No doubt ye've read all the
               nonsense in the newspapers?

STARR: Well, they do seem to be splashing it about a
               bit, don't they?

McCRAW: I tell ye, Mike – it's a real headache! A first-
               class headache!

STARR: Well, supposing you tell me your side of the
               story. Start at the beginning.

McCRAW: Well ... I don't know whether ye ever met Lord
               Harringson, but ...

STARR: No, I'm afraid I didn't. The old boy was getting
               on, wasn't he?

McCRAW: Eight-two. (*Thoughtfully*) Yes, he was a grand old rascal! (*Suddenly*) Well, Mike ... every Saturday morning Lord Harringson used to visit the Medusa Club in Pall Mall. He usually arrived there at about half past ten. He used to pull a huge armchair up to the fireplace, sit down with a copy of Pickwick ... and he never used to budge until about ... Oh, six or seven o'clock in the evening.

STARR: But what about lunch?

McCRAW: It never used to trouble the old boy. Occasionally he had a sandwich or two. Well, last Saturday morning his Lordship arrived at the Club at about his usual time. He pulled the armchair up to the fireplace and started to read his book. No one spoke to him, no one disturbed him ... as a matter of fact the Club was pretty deserted all day.

STARR: (*Interested*) Go on.

McCRAW: Well, at about half past three in the afternoon a Steward – a chappie by the name o' Pitman – suddenly noticed that the old boy had dropped his book. He went across to the chair, picked it up, and then got the shock of his life ... Lord Harringson was dead.

STARR: M'm.

McCRAW: The Steward sent for the Secretary and the Secretary sent for the club doctor. The doctor examined his Lordship and expressed the opinion that ... he'd been ... poisoned. Our man confirms this.

STARR: M'm. Did his Lordship have anything to drink at the club?

McCRAW: Not a thing.

STARR:	Anything to eat?
McCRAW:	No.
STARR:	Could he have taken the poison prior to …
McCRAW:	Prior to his arrival at the Medusa? No. No, impossible. Both doctors confirmed this.
STARR:	M'm – did you search his Lordship?
McCRAW:	Aye – everything's here, Mike.

We hear the noise of a drawer opening.

McCRAW:	Copy of The Pickwick Papers … Saturday's Daily Gazette which the old boy was sitting on … his watch chain … watch … small pen knife … diary … wallet … two letters … pipe … tobacco pouch … box o' matches … oh, and a cigarette lighter which doesn't work.
STARR:	I see the watch is stopped at a quarter to eleven.
McCRAW:	Aye – it wants re-winding.
STARR:	M'm. I'd like to have a look at the Club, Robert – and I'd also like to have a word with the Secretary.
McCRAW:	His name's Lester. Ye'll find him quite helpful but a shade pedantic. Still, I suppose that isn't surprising really when ye come to consider the sort o' life that the …

FADE SCENE.

FADE IN MICHAEL STARR.

STARR:	I take it that this is the room, Mr Lester, in which …
LESTER:	(*Interrupting STARR*) Yes. Yes, Mr Starr. This is the very room. That's the chair in which his Lordship was sitting – the one in the corner.
STARR:	M'm. I see you've got a sort of cocktail bar at the end of the room.

LESTER:	Yes. Not a very edifying spectacle, I'm afraid, but we've had to cut down on our staff and it – well, it does help a great deal.
STARR:	Who's in charge of the bar?
LESTER:	One of the Stewards – actually the – er – fellow who discovered Lord Harringson.
McCRAW:	Pitman.
LESTER:	Yes, Inspector – Wilfrid Pitman.
STARR:	I'd like a word with him.
LESTER:	He should be here any minute, sir.
STARR:	Mr Lester, tell me ... did you actually see Lord Harringson arrive on Saturday morning?
LESTER:	No. When I saw him he was already sitting in the chair ... reading.
STARR:	What time was that?
LESTER:	Now let me see ... I brought the morning papers in with me ... they were rather late ... it was about, er ... oh, a quarter to twelve.
STARR:	Did you speak to his Lordship?
LESTER:	No. No, I just put the paper down, had a word with Pitman, and ... then ... left ... (*Suddenly*) Oh, here is Pitman now.
STARR:	Good.
LESTER:	Will you excuse me, Inspector?
McCRAW:	Aye. Aye, that's all right, Mr Lester.
PITMAN:	You wanted to see me, Inspector?
McCRAW:	Mr Starr here would like to ask ye a few questions.
STARR:	Did you see Lord Harringson arrive on Saturday morning?
PITMAN:	Yes, sir.
STARR:	What was he carrying?
PITMAN:	Why, just 'is copy of Pickwick Papers, sir.
STARR:	What time was that?

PITMAN:	About half past ten, sir.
STARR:	Did Lord Harringson have anything to drink at all?
PITMAN:	No, sir. I never went near 'im until I picked the book up.
STARR:	You didn't serve him with a drink?
PITMAN:	No, sir.
STARR:	He didn't – er – cross over to the cocktail bar at any time?
PITMAN:	He never got out of 'is chair, sir – from the moment he arrived. If he 'ad 'ave done I'd 'ave seen him – couldn't 'ave 'elped but 'ave seen him. I was in the blinkin' room all the time.
STARR:	Mr Lester came into the lounge at about a quarter to twelve – did he speak to Lord Harringson?
PITMAN:	No, sir.
STARR:	(*Dismissing PITMAN*) Right. Thank you, Pitman. That's all.
PITMAN:	Thank you, sir.
McCRAW:	(*Quietly*) Well, Mike – what do you make of things?
STARR:	(*Elated*) We've got him! We've got him, Robert my lad!
McCRAW:	Got him? Why – why, who do ye mean, laddie?
STARR:	Don't be silly, Bob! (*Seriously*) The man who murdered Lord Harringson.

FADE UP of music.
FADE DOWN.

ANNOUNCER:	Do you know who murdered Lord Harringson? Later in the programme we

shall return you to Michael Starr for the solution to tonight's detective problem.

Turn over for the solution to mystery sixteen.

MYSTERY SIXTEEN – THE SOLUTION

ANNOUNCER: We now return you to Michael Starr for the solution to tonight's detective problem.

McCRAW: Got him? Why – why, who do ye mean, laddie?

STARR: Don't be silly, Bob! (*Seriously*) The man who murdered Lord Harringson.

McCRAW: Ye mean to say ye know who murdered Lord Harringson?

STARR: Of course I do! Don't you?

McCRAW: I'm blowed if I do!

STARR: Well, it's really quite simple, Inspector. You see, Pitman happens to be lying …

McCRAW: How do ye know he's lying?

STARR: For the simple reason that Lord Harringson did get out of his chair.

McCRAW: He did!

STARR: Yes, and ten to one he crossed over to the cocktail bar.

McCRAW: But, Mike – how do you know?

STARR: Don't you remember what the Secretary said? He said he arrived at a quarter to twelve with the morning papers.

McCRAW: Well?

STARR: At a quarter to twelve Lord Harringson was already sitting in the chair.

McCRAW: WELL?

STARR: Well, if his Lordship never got out of the chair how the devil did you happen to find him sitting on a copy of the Morning Gazette?

McCRAW: Well, I'll be … be …

STARR: Exactly!
FADE UP of music.

MYSTERY SEVENTEEN
Cast:

Michael Starr . . . . Henry Oscar

Inspector McCraw . . . . Ian Sadler

Sgt Marshall . . . . Fred Yule

Mrs Nora Grant . . . . Rita Vale

As the opening music finishes CROSS FADE to INSPECTOR MCCRAW.

McCRAW: (*Slowly*) Well … what do ye think of it, Mike?

STARR: (*Quietly*) It's pretty good … you'd never dream it was counterfeit.

McCRAW: Feel the paper! It's just like a real pound note! And, man, just look at the lettering … it's absolutely identical!

STARR: Yes … it's certainly a first-class piece of work. Where did you get this?

McCRAW: (*Amazed*) Where did we get it? Why, man, the whole bl … blinkin' town's snowed under with 'em. D'you know how many we picked up on Saturday, Mike? Three hundred and fifty! Three hundred and fifty, laddie!

STARR: I take it things are getting serious?

McCRAW: Serious! Why, man, if it's wasn't for me strong constitution I don't know what on earth I should …

STARR: (*Interrupting McCRAW on the word 'strong'. Still looking at a note*) Hello!

McCRAW: (*Quickly*) What is it?

STARR: (*Slowly*) Do you know, Inspector … I've got a hunch about this business … I've got a queer sort of feeling that … there's a woman behind it.

McCRAW: (*Staggered*) Now that's mighty funny, Mike! That's mighty funny!

STARR: Why do you say that?

McCRAW: Listen laddie! On Saturday afternoon, at Moorfield races three hundred and fifty of these notes were passed. We've checked up on all the bookmakers and we've come to the

	conclusion that the notes were passed, not by a syndicate as we originally suspected, but by a single individual.
STARR:	And you suspect?
McCRAW:	(*Tensely*) We suspect a woman, Mike. A woman by the name of Grant … Mrs Nora Grant.
STARR:	Go on.
McCRAW:	I telephoned through to Mrs Grant this morning and had a chat with her. She's calling round to see me this afternoon. Now this is the extraordinary thing, Mike! Mrs Grant swears that she wasn't at the Moorfield races on Saturday but that she spent the afternoon at the Rexton meeting.
STARR:	Rexton? That's the other side of London.
McCRAW:	Exactly!
STARR:	Can she prove that she went to the Rexton races?
McCRAW:	I rather think she can, Mike. But what's more to the point – we can't prove she didn't!
STARR:	(*Thoughtfully*) Mrs Nora Grant … the name seems familiar. She's a Canadian, isn't she?
McCRAW:	Aye! Quite a character. We've had our eye on her for some little time.

There is a knock on the door and the door opens.

MARSHALL:	You sent for me, Inspector?
McCRAW:	(*Suddenly*) Ah, yes, laddie! Come in! Come in! Mike, do ye know Sergeant Marshall?
STARR:	Yes! Yes, of course. How are you, sergeant?
MARSHALL:	Nicely, thank you, sir.
McCRAW:	Sergeant, I'm given to understand that last Saturday afternoon you were off duty and that you went to Rexton races – is that correct?

MARSHALL: That's correct, sir. I caught the 12.35 from Four Trees an' was just in time to miss the first race. And did I feel like a piece of chewed string!

STARR: Why? Was it a tedious journey?

MARSHALL: No, I wouldn't say that, sir, but the train didn't stop at all, there wasn't a corridor, and the blinkin' carriage was packed. And then to pile the misery on, as you might say, I'd picked the winner of the first race an' was too late to back it.

STARR: (*Laughing*) Oh, I see.

McCRAW: Sergeant, tell me – do you know a woman called Grant … Mrs Nora Grant?

MARSHALL: Why, yes, sir. She doesn't live very far from our place. A Canadian lady?

McCRAW: Aye! Aye, that's right! Do you know her to speak to?

MARSHALL: Er – no, sir. Only by sight.

McCRAW: You didn't see her on Saturday … at Rexton … by any chance?

MARSHALL: (*Thoughtfully*) No. No, I can't say I did, sir.

A telephone rings.

McCRAW: (*Dismissing MARSHALL*) Right! Thank ye, sergeant!

McCRAW lifts the telephone receiver.

McCRAW: (*On the phone*) Hello? … Yes … yes … Oh, thank you … We'll be down right away!

The receiver is replaced.

McCRAW: Mrs Grant's here, Mike. She's in the Superintendent's office.

STARR: Good. I'd like to have a word with her.

McCRAW: You know, the thing that baffles me about this business is the extraordinary manner in which so many …

FADE SCENE.

FADE IN NORA GRANT.

NORA: Why, this is really quite ridiculous! To accuse me of passing counterfeit notes, why … why, I've never heard of anything so … so fantastic in all my life!

McCRAW: Ye don't understand us, Mrs Grant. We don't accuse you of anything. We are simply trying to …

STARR: (*Pleasantly*) If you were at Rexton races on Saturday afternoon, madam, then it's quite obvious that you didn't pass the bank notes.

NORA: The notes, I take it, were passed at the …

STARR: At the Moorfield meeting.

NORA: I haven't been to Moorfield for ages. As a matter of fact I'm not very keen on it. It's always so dreadfully crowded – although I must confess Rexton wasn't exactly deserted.

STARR: How did you get to Rexton – by train?

NORA: Yes, I caught the 12.35 from Four Trees. That's our local station. (*Pleasantly*) As a matter of fact I saw a colleague of yours, Inspector … Sergeant – er – Sergeant Marshall. (*With a little laugh*) Unfortunately, I don't think he noticed me.

STARR: Was the train crowded?

NORA: Oh, frightfully! I had to travel part of the way in a non-smoker which infuriated me!

STARR: Did you arrive in time for the first race?

NORA: No, unfortunately we just missed it.

STARR:	I see. (*Dismissing NORA*) Well, thank you, Mrs Grant.
McCRAW:	This way, madam!

The door opens and closes.

McCRAW:	Well, Mike, what do ye think?
STARR:	(*With authority*) She passed the notes all right. There's no doubt about that!
McCRAW:	But how the Dickens could she if she went to Rexton?
STARR:	That's just the point, Bob, she didn't go to Rexton!
McCRAW:	(*Astonished*) She didn't go to Rexton? Now – how do ye know?

FADE UP of music.
FADE DOWN.

ANNOUNCER:	Why does Michael Starr suspect Nora Grant? Do you know? Later in the programme you will hear from Michael Starr himself the solution to tonight's detective problem.

MYSTERY SEVENTEEN – THE SOLUTION

ANNOUNCER: We now return you to Michael Starr for the solution to tonight's detective problem.

STARR: That's just the point, Bob, she didn't go to Rexton!

McCRAW: (*Astonished*) She didn't go to Rexton? Now – how do ye know?

STARR: (*Laughing*) My dear Robert, you didn't swallow that nonsense about her seeing Marshall, did you? You can take it from me, she didn't see Sergeant Marshall for the simple reason that she wasn't on the train.

McCRAW: How do ye know that she wasn't on the train?

STARR: Didn't you hear what she said? "I had to travel part of the way in a non-smoker". Implying that during the course of the journey she changed her compartment.

McCRAW: Well?

STARR: How could she change her compartment? The train didn't stop and there wasn't a corridor!!

McCRAW: Well, I'll be … Mike, you're a genius! Man, you're a wizard!

STARR: (*Quietly*) Yes, but I'm awfully worried, Bob.

McCRAW: (*Deeply concerned*) Why, man, what is it?

STARR: (*Pulling McCRAW's leg – imitating his accent*) It's me constitution …

STARR laughs.
FADE UP of music.

MYSTERY EIGHTEEN
Cast:

Michael Starr . . . . Henry Oscar

Inspector McCraw . . . . Ian Sadler

Mary . . . . Lucille Lisle

As the opening music finishes CROSS FADE to a door opening. There are background noises of a typical country lane.

MARY: (*A tense whisper*) Eric! Eric, where are you? (*Tensely – surprised*) Oh, there you are! I got your note ... what do you want? Eric, why did you choose this place, it's so deserted and ... (*Impatiently*) Now don't be silly, darling ... don't stand there staring, I ... I ... (*Frightened*) Eric! Eric, what do you want? (*Terrified*) Put ... put that gun down; don't be silly, because ... (*She screams*)

We hear the noise of a revolver shot. A man laughs, sinister, uncontrolled laughter.

FADE SCENE.

FADE UP the sound of water being splashed and a tap running into a bath.

McCRAW: (*Exasperated*) Mike! For the last time ... for the last time, laddie ... are ye goin' to help me, or are ye going to persist in ...

STARR: (*Pleasantly – interrupting McCRAW*) Pass the soap, old boy!

McCRAW: (*Finally exasperated*) Mike, I'm in a quandary!

STARR: (*Completely matter of fact*) Yes, and I'm in the bath, old boy!

McCRAW: (*Desperately*) Laddie, I don't think ye understand! If I don't solve this case then the Assistant Commissioner has threatened to ...

STARR: (*Casually – interrupting McCRAW again*) I say, pass me that sponge, old boy!

McCRAW: The sponge, why certain ... (*Suddenly exasperated*) Holy smoke!

STARR:	(*Chuckling*) What is it? What's all the excitement about?
McCRAW:	Ye know perfectly well what the excitement's about!
STARR:	The Whitehouse case?
McCRAW:	(*Depressed*) Aye.
STARR:	Well, supposing you tell me all about it, Robert – right from the beginning. And don't catch your elbow on that tap or you'll turn the shower on yourself!
McCRAW:	What? Oh, yes … Well, exactly a fortnight ago today a girl by the name o' Mary Whitehouse was found murdered in a small, deserted bungalow on the outskirts of Little Frampton.
STARR:	How was she murdered, Bob?
McCRAW:	She was shot. Now the motive seems to be pretty clear, Mike. Mary Whitehouse was engaged to a fellow by the name of Eric Gleason: three months ago she broke off the engagement. Gleason, who seems to be rather an excitable sort o' chappie, threatened to murder her. Naturally, as soon as we heard this we tried to get hold of Gleason, but … he disappeared. Sergeant Saunders picked him up this morning, however, in a public house just outside of Croydon.
STARR:	Have you spoken to Gleason?
McCRAW:	Aye.
STARR:	What reason does he give for … disappearing?
McCRAW:	The obvious reason. He says that he knew he would automatically come under suspicion, and … well, to put it bluntly, the laddie got scared.
STARR:	M'm – do <u>you</u> think Gleason committed the murder?

McCRAW: Aye, I think he did, Mike. But I don't see how we are going to prove it. You see, according to the doctor who examined the body, Mary Whitehouse was shot at about a quarter to two.

STARR: Well?

McCRAW: Well, Gleason's got an alibi. As a matter of fact he's given me a detailed account of exactly what he did from ten o'clock in the morning.

STARR: Have you checked up on it?

McCRAW: Not yet: I haven't had time. But it's genuine enough – you can see that at a glance. At ten o'clock, for instance, he went over to see an aunt of his at Lower Frampton. He was back at about a quarter to one. Shortly after lunch he went round to the bank and cashed a cheque. At a quarter past two he went to the local cinema and came out at about half past four. He had a spot of tea in the village and was back in the house at about a quarter to six.

STARR: M'm.

McCRAW: (*Deeply concerned*) Mike ...

STARR: Yes?

McCRAW: Mike, I wish ye'd get out of the bath and give this matter your serious consideration, why man if I ...

STARR: (*Laughing*) Don't be silly, old boy! This is so simple I don't even have to get out of the bath!

McCRAW: What! Simple! Why man, what on earth are ye talking about, and don't give me a ...

FADE UP of music.
FADE DOWN.

ANNOUNCER: What makes Michael Starr suspect Eric Gleason? Do you know? Later in the programme you will hear from Michael Starr himself the solution to tonight's detective problem.

Turn over the page to find the solution to mystery eighteen.

MYSTERY EIGHTEEN – THE SOLUTION

ANNOUNCER: We now return you to Michael Starr for the solution to tonight's detective problem.

STARR: (*Laughing*) Don't be silly, old boy! This is so simple I don't even have to get out of the bath!

McCRAW: What! Simple! Why man, what on earth are ye talking about, and don't give me a …

STARR: (*Interrupting McCRAW – amused*) Robert, you really are a chump!

McCRAW: What do you mean?

STARR: Just look at that statement of Gleason's! It's a pack of lies from start to finish. (*Imitating McCRAW*) Shortly after lunch he went round to the bank and cashed a cheque …

McCRAW: Well?

STARR: Well, how could he cash a cheque at his bank – a fortnight today? It was Whit Monday!

McCRAW: Well, I'll be …

The sound of the shower is heard.

McCRAW: Mike! Mike! You've turned the shower on me!

STARR: And you deserve it, Robert, my lad! You deserve it!

FADE UP of music.

MYSTERY NINETEEN
Cast:

Michael Starr . . . . Henry Oscar

Inspector McCraw . . . . Ian Sadler

Janet Dawson . . . . .Grizelda Hervey

Dr Elkwood . . . . .Cyril Gardiner

After opening music finishes CROSS FADE to a door opening.

STARR: (*Surprised*) Why, hello, Bob!

The door closes.

McCRAW: (*Suddenly*) Good gracious me, is that a mirage I'm seeing, Mike – or is it really a bottle of Scotch?

STARR: (*Amused*) Would you like a drink?

McCRAW: Aye!

STARR: What'll you have? I can recommend the brandy.

McCRAW: That bottle o' Scotch looks awfully tempting!

STARR: (*Confidentially*) Try the brandy, old boy. It's absolutely first class.

McCRAW: (*Smacking his lips*) Well – er ...

STARR: Brandy?

McCRAW: Er – it seems an awful pity to waste brandy on a Scotsman!

STARR: (*Laughing*) O.K. Robert!

STARR pours the drink.

STARR: Water ... or soda?

McCRAW: Just a wee ... wee ... drop o' ... Whoa! Whoa!

STARR: (*Laughs. After a moment*) Cheerio!

McCRAW: Cheerio! (*He smacks his lips*) Ah! That's a lot better!

STARR: You haven't answered my question, Bob.

McCRAW: What question? (*Suddenly*) Oh, yes! Do ye happen to know a Mr and Mrs Bernard C Dawson, by any chance?

STARR: Yes. I know them. They've got a flat on the third floor.

McCRAW: That's right.

STARR: Mrs Dawson's rather a good looking woman, isn't she?

177

McCRAW:	Aye, quite pretty in a picture postcard sort o' way.
STARR:	There was some talk about her being friendly with that actor chappie – er – what's his name?
McCRAW:	(*Quietly – surprised*) Derek Walton?
STARR:	(*Casually*) Yes. Yes, that's right. (*After a moment*) Why – what's the matter, Bob? What's happened?
McCRAW:	Well, about half an hour ago, just as I was leaving the Yard, I received a telephone call. It was from a Dr Elkwood and he said he was speaking on behalf of a Mrs Bernard C Dawson.
STARR:	Elkwood? (*Thoughtfully*) Elkwood? Yes, I think that's her brother.
McCRAW:	Aye, that's right. Well, the chappie sounded pretty urgent so I agreed to pop round to the flat straight away. When I arrived here they took me …
STARR:	They?
McCRAW:	Mrs Dawson and the doctor.
STARR:	Yes, go on.
McCRAW:	They took me down to one of those small lock-up garages at the back of the mews.
STARR:	Yes, Dawson keeps his car there, I believe.
McCRAW:	Aye, the poor devil keeps his car there all right. Dawson was laid out on the floor o' the garage with his head propped up against the exhaust pipe o' the car.
STARR:	Dead?
McCRAW:	Aye! According to the doctor he'd been dead a couple o' hours or more. There doesn't seem to be any doubt about what actually happened. Dawson obviously shut himself in the garage,

started the car up, then made himself as comfortable as possible with his face turned towards the exhaust pipe. The doctor's report confirms this: the poor devil died from asphyxiation. (*After a moment*) He wasn't a pleasant sight, Mike. If it hadn't been for my strong constitution I don't really know what I should …

STARR: (*On the word 'constitution'*) Yes. Well, it seems like a perfectly straight forward case of suicide, Bob.

McCRAW: Yes. Yes … I think so.

STARR: What do you mean you <u>think</u> so?

McCRAW: (*Quietly*) Well – when I examined Dawson I noticed on his wrists a sort of – er – well … mark: it looked to me rather as if his hands had been tied together.

STARR: M'm.

McCRAW: Now, if his hands had been tied together, he might even have been gagged as well, in which case …

STARR: (*Quietly*) In which case Dawson might have been taken down to the garage and deliberately held with his face turned towards …

McCRAW: Exactly!

STARR: Has anything been touched in the garage?

McCRAW: No – not a thing. I've put Sergeant Miller on guard. Oh – the body's been moved upstairs to the flat.

STARR: Where's Mrs Dawson?

McCRAW: Well, when I left her she was in the garage talking to this doctor fellow.

STARR: I see. Well, come along, Bob. I'd rather like a word with Mrs Dawson. (*Confidentially*) You

179

know, the point that intrigues me about this case is the fact that judging from the details …

FADE SCENE.

FADE In MICHAEL STARR.

STARR: Tell me, who discovered Mr Dawson?

JANET: I – I found Bernard. I came down here to get the car and … well … there he was … poor darling!

STARR: Did you know that your husband was in the garage?

JANET: Good gracious me, no! I – I thought Bernard was still at the office. He hardly ever leaves the office much before six.

STARR: Mrs Dawson, forgive me if I ask you a rather personal question, but … were you on very friendly terms with your husband?

JANET: (*Indignantly*) Why – why yes, of course! How dare you insinuate that …

ELKWOOD: (*Interrupting JANET*) Janet. My dear, it's not a bit of use losing your temper! Mr Starr and the Inspector are simply doing their duty. They are here to help you, and if you don't intend to tell them the truth then I'm afraid that I must.

JANET: What do you mean?

ELKWOOD: We all know that you didn't get along very well with Bernard. The whole family knows it, and sooner or later the police are bound to hear …

JANET: (*Obviously distressed*) It's all very well for you, Walter. It's all very well for you to be smug and self-satisfied. But you don't know what I've had to contend with during the past four years. You only knew Bernard from … from the outside! He was quite a different person when one really got to know him! He was mean ... and cruel ... and callous ... and ... (*She is almost crying*)

STARR: (*Softly*) Mrs Dawson ...

McCRAW: Now lassie ...

ELKWOOD: Janet, please!

JANET: I'm – I'm sorry.

STARR: Mrs Dawson, you were saying ... you came down here to get the car.

JANET: Oh – yes. Mr Walton rang up at about five and asked if he could borrow the car. I – I said yes, and offered to take it down to him.

STARR: That's Mr Derek Walton, the actor?

JANET: Yes. He's – he's rather a friend of mine.

ELKWOOD: I expect Derek's still waiting for it, darling. Shall I take it down to him? (*Suddenly*) Oh, er – are we allowed to move the car, Inspector?

McCRAW: Yes, that'll be all right, doctor.

JANET: No! Do – I'll take it down, Walter. I – I want to see Derek. I ...

ELKWOOD: (*Sharply*) Now don't be silly, Janet. You're not in a condition to drive.

JANET: (*Tensely*) I shall be all right! Don't worry – I shall be – all right.

ELKWOOD: (*Impatiently*) T't! T't!

The car engine turns over once or twice but refuses to start.

JANET: (*Very flustered*) Oh dear! Oh, dear! Now what's happened! I'm sure the car is perfectly all right because ...

ELKWOOD: (*Quietly – controlling his exasperation*) It won't start if you don't switch on, Janet!

JANET: Oh! Oh, yes ... of course!

McCRAW laughs.

ELKWOOD: You really ought not to drive the ...

181

JANET: I tell you I'm all right, Walter! Leave me
                alone!

The car starts and drives out of the garage.

ELKWOOD: Oh dear! I do hope that she'll take care!

STARR: Don't worry, doctor. She'll be all right.
                Come along, Bob, we'd better go back to
                the flat. You'd better come along too, doctor
                – you look as if you can do with a drink.

ELKWOOD: Well, to tell you the truth I think perhaps I
                could use one. This business has rather
                shaken me up you know. I'm very fond of
                Janet and I was quite fond of old Walter, as
                much as one can be fond of a fellow with
                that ...

FADE SCENE.

CROSS FADE to a door opening.

STARR: Ah, here we are! Well, what do you feel
                like, sir?

ELKWOOD: May I have a whisky and soda?

STARR: Certainly! Inspector?

McCRAW: (*Perplexed*) Mike! Mike, tell me ... is it
                suicide ... or murder?

ELKWOOD: Why don't be stupid, Inspector! It's
                obviously a perfectly straight forward case
                of suicide!

STARR: On the contrary, doctor – it's obviously a
                perfectly straightforward case of ... murder!

FADE UP of music.
FADE DOWN.

ANNOUNCER: How does Michael Starr know that Bernard
                C. Dawson was murdered? Later in the
                programme you will hear from Michael

Starr himself the solution to tonight's detective problem.

MYSTERY NINETEEN – THE SOLUTION

ANNOUNCER: We now return you to Michael Starr for the solution to tonight's detective problem.

STARR: On the contrary, doctor – it's obviously a perfectly straightforward case of ... murder!

ELKWOOD: What – what do you mean, sir?

STARR: Before Mrs Dawson was able to drive the car out of the garage she had to switch the car on, but don't you realise that if Dawson had committed suicide then the car would never have been switched off? It would simply have 'knocked out'. The poor devil couldn't very well commit suicide and then get up and switch the ignition off, now could he?

McCRAW: Good Lord, no! No, of course not!

ELKWOOD: Good heavens, no! (*Without thinking*) what a fool! I should never have ...

STARR: (*Quickly*) You should never have switched the car off after you'd made it look as if Dawson had committed suicide! Exactly!!

ELKWOOD: Why, you dirty ...

STARR: Oh, no you don't, my friend!

McCRAW: Look out, Mike!

We hear a thud and a cry from ELKWOOD.

McCRAW: Oh, nice work, laddie! Nice work!

STARR: Are you all right, Robert?

McCRAW: (*Breathlessly*) Aye ... aye, I'm all right!

STARR: I daresay you could do with another whisky and soda!

McCRAW: (*Weakly*) If it's all the same to you, laddie – I'll try the brandy!

STARR: (*Laughing*) Oh! Oh! What a constitution!
FADE UP of music.

MYSTERY TWENTY
Cast:

Michael Starr . . . . Henry Oscar
Inspector McCraw . . . . Ian Sadler
Ted Cross . . . . Fred Yule
Fred Smith . . . . .John Rorke
Dorman . . . . Arthur Ridley

As the opening music finishes CROSS FADE to typical background noises of a railway station.

DORMAN: (*A cultured serious voice*) Is this the luggage depot?

TED: (*Cockney, cheerful*) This is it, guv'nor.

DORMAN: Well, I should like to leave this case here, if I may? I'll pick it up at about half past five.

TED: (*Raising his voice*) Will you be 'ere after five, Fred?

FRED: Yes, Ted!

TED: That's o.k., mister – 'ere's your ticket.

DORMAN: Thank you.

FRED: (*After a pause*) Miserable lookin' blighter!

TED: 'E didn't look too 'appy, did 'e? Where shall we put it?

FRED: We'd better put it on the ... (*Surprised*) What's up, Ted?

TED: (*Amused*) Blimey, this 'ere case must be full of alarm clocks! (*He laughs*)

FRED: How do you know?

TED: Listen! (*Highly amused*) You can 'ear 'em. Tick-tock, tick-tock, tick-tock, tick-tock!

FRED: (*Also amused*) Ha! Well, I'm blowed.

TED: (*Wishfully*) Could do with a new alarm.

FRED: Me too.

A pause.

TED: (*Thoughtfully, but not perturbed*) They seem funny sort of things to carry about, Fred.

FRED: That's what I was thinking.

TED: (*Amused*) You can't 'alf 'ear 'em ... tick-tock, tick-tock, tick-tock!

FRED: I suppose it couldn't be anything else? There's nothing else wot goes tick-tock, tick-tock, is there, Ted?

TED: No … only an alarm … (*Completely matter of fact*) … and a bomb of course!

FRED: Yus, well we're not expecting … WHAT!!!!

TED: Cor' blimey!!!!

FADE UP station noises and excited voices then FADE SCENE.

FADE UP excited voices of INSPECTOR McCRAW, TED, FRED, and MICHAEL STARR, all talking at once.

STARR: (*Raising his voice above the rabble*) Gentlemen! Gentlemen, please!

The voices die down slightly.

STARR: For goodness sake, let's get this straightened out! Now come on, Bob, what's it all about?

McCRAW: (*Exasperated*) Mike! Mike, I'm bewildered, I'm confused, I'm astonished, I'm mortified, I'm speechless, I'm … Why, man, if it wasn't for me strong constitution, I'd …

TED and FRED suddenly burst into animated conversation – the rabble starts all over again.

STARR: (*With great authority*) Gentlemen!!!

There is silence.

STARR: (*Almost with menace*) Now, Bob, I'm going to give you ten seconds … ten seconds in which to tell me … exactly … what … it's … all … about!!!

McCRAW: (*After a deep breath*) These two gentlemen, Mike – Mr Ted Cross and Mr Fred Smith, look after the left luggage office at Westmoreland Street Station. Yesterday afternoon a man deposited a suitcase there containing a bomb, by a miracle …

FRED: By a sheer blinking miracle we escaped …

McCRAW:	But the bomb did quite a lot of damage, Mike. Now the point is this …
STARR:	The point is – WHO deposited the suitcase?
McCRAW:	Exactly!
STARR:	Well, have you any suspects?
McCRAW:	Yes, a man called Dorman. He's downstairs now in the Assistant Commissioner's office.
STARR:	Have these fellows seen him?
FRED:	Aye, we 'ad a decko at 'im a few minutes ago.
McCRAW:	Without the laddie knowing.
STARR:	Did you recognise him?
TED:	It isn't the same bloke wot deposited …
McCRAW:	(*Interrupting*) I wouldn't be too sure, laddie. Dorman's a past master at disguise.
STARR:	What was the man like who deposited the suitcase?
TED:	Oh, fairly tall …
FRED:	Bit on the short side …
TED:	Dark …
FRED:	Oh, I don't know about dark …
STARR:	Clean shaven?
FRED:	(*Thoughtfully*) Er … yes …
TED:	No, he'd a bit of a 'Charley', Fred.
STARR:	(*Exasperated*) Did he walk on two legs???
FRED:	(*Seriously*) Oh, yes.
TED:	Oh, yus. Yes, he walked on two legs!
STARR:	Well, that's something! Come on, Bob. I want a word with this Mr Dorman.
McCRAW:	You'll find him a rather self-possessed sort o' cove if I'm any judge of …

FADE SCENE.

FADE IN of DORMAN.

DORMAN: (*Calmly*) Now look, Inspector, what is all this nonsense?

McCRAW: We have reason to believe, sir, that you deposited a suitcase at Westmoreland Street Station yesterday afternoon. The suitcase in question contained a bomb, and ...

DORMAN: Why – why, this is fantastic! I – I never went near Westmoreland Street Station yesterday afternoon. As a matter of fact I've never even been in that particular station!

STARR: (*Quietly*) Can you prove that you didn't deposit the suitcase?

DORMAN: Of course I can prove it! (*Acidly*) But what's more to the point, can you prove that I did, Mr Starr?

McCRAW: (*Clearing his throat*) Hum!

STARR: (*Quietly*) That remains to be seen.

DORMAN: Look here, take me down to the station and let the – er – porter fellow have a look at me. If he recognises me then I'm obviously your man. If not – then it's quite obvious that I'm innocent.

STARR: There's no need to take you down to the station. Fred Smith and Mr Cross, the porters concerned, are already here – at Scotland Yard.

DORMAN: Then bring them in!

STARR: One moment! (*With authority*) You say you never went near Westmoreland Street Station yesterday afternoon?

DORMAN: No, I spent the afternoon at Richmond.

STARR: Alone?

DORMAN: No, with a friend of mine. A girl called Iris Black.

STARR: How did you get to Richmond?

DORMAN: We cycled.

STARR:	M'm – that's interesting. Tell me, how long did it …
DORMAN:	(*Impatiently interrupting STARR*) Oh, don't give me this Sherlock Holmes nonsense, please! Let's be perfectly straight about this matter.
STARR:	(*Quietly*) What do you suggest?
DORMAN:	(*Almost exasperated*) I suggest that you bring in the two porters you mentioned – Mr Smith and Ted Cross – and see if they recognise me.
STARR:	And supposing they don't?
DORMAN:	Then it's quite obvious that I'm innocent.
STARR:	Yes, but – I happen to know that you're not innocent, Mr Dorman.
DORMAN:	(*Superciliously*) Yes. Yes, but can you prove it, Mr Starr?
STARR:	As a matter of fact … I … think … I … can!
McCRAW:	WHAT!!!

FADE UP of music.
FADE DOWN.

ANNOUNCER:	What makes Michael Starr suspect Dorman? Do you know? Later in the programme you will hear from Michael Starr himself the solution to tonight's detective problem.

MYSTERY TWENTY – THE SOLUTION

ANNOUNCER: We now return you to Michael Starr for the solution to tonight's detective problem.

STARR: As a matter of fact ... I ... think ... I ... can.

McCRAW: WHAT!!!

STARR: Mr Dorman, would you mind explaining something to me?

DORMAN: Well?

STARR: Tell me, how did you know that they called one of the porters <u>TED</u> Cross?

DORMAN: Why – why, you said so!

STARR: Oh no, I didn't! I said Fred Smith and Mr Cross.

DORMAN: (*Without thinking*) Well, I must have overheard the other fellow call him Ted when I handed ... (*Suddenly – exasperated*) Why ... you ... you ... dirty ... double crossing ...

McCRAW: Look out, Mike!!!

We hear a loud smack followed by a groan and a thud.

McCRAW: Oh, nice work, laddie! Nice work! But it's a good job you ducked!

STARR: You're telling me!

STARR laughs.

FADE UP of music.

MYSTERY TWENTY-ONE
Cast:

As the opening music finishes CROSS FADE to a door opening.

STARR: Sorry I'm late, Inspector! I was out of Town when your message came through and ... (*Surprised*) Hello! What's the matter? You look worried!

McCRAW: I feel worried, Mike! I've had the Home Office twisting my tail all the morning!

STARR: What is it, Bob? What's it all about?

McCRAW: Well, I don't have to tell you, laddie, that the County of Redfordshire is a prohibited area and just at the moment they don't want a lot of strangers poking their noses into – er – ....

STARR: Affairs which don't concern them?

McCRAW: Exactly! Well, Mike, two or three weeks ago we had reasons to suspect that information of a rather important nature was .... (*He pauses*)

STARR: (*Seriously*) ... was being transmitted from Redfordshire?

McCRAW: Yes!

STARR: Go on, Bob ...

McCRAW: I sent a man down there to investigate. Chappie by the name of Foster. That was on the – er – twenty seventh of last month.

STARR: Well?

McCRAW: We haven't heard a word from him since, Mike! He was supposed to contact the local police straight away but they never so much as set eyes on him.

STARR: What sort of a man is Foster?

McCRAW: Thoroughly reliable! One of the best youngsters we've got.

STARR: Where was he supposed to stay – at Redford?

McCRAW: Aye. We booked him a room at The White Horse but he never checked in.

STARR: M'm …

A telephone rings.

McCRAW: Excuse me! (*He lifts the receiver*) Hello? … Yes, Inspector McCraw speaking … (*To STARR*) This must be urgent, Mike! It's the River Patrol! (*On the phone*) Hello … Yes, I'm listening … (*Softly*) When? … Are they sure it's Foster? … I see … Thank ye for ringing! (*He replaces the receiver*)

STARR: What's happened?

McCRAW: We've found Foster! The River Patrol picked his body out of the Thames twenty minutes ago.

STARR: Murder?

McCRAW: Aye! Aye, it's murder all right! (*Suddenly*) Mike! Mike! Somewhere in Redfordshire, in a secret hideout, there is a man … A dangerous man … and we've got to find him!

STARR: M'm – who's in charge of the case down there?

McCRAW: The Chief Constable of the County … fellow by the name of Colonel Sandown. Most reliable fellow; knows every inch of the County.

STARR: What made you say, just now, that this man – the man you're looking for – has a secret hideout?

McCRAW: He must have a secret hideout, Mike – otherwise Colonel Sandown would have laid hands on him. I tell ye, the Chief Constable knows every village, and every stone in the place.

STARR: Have you met Colonel Sandown – personally, I mean?

McCRAW: Aye! I've known him off and on for many years. Charming fellow! Doesn't enjoy the best of health though, I'm afraid.

STARR: When are you going down to Redfordshire again?

McCRAW: Tomorrow afternoon, on the two-thirty … Can you make it?

STARR: (*Thoughtfully; intrigued*) Yes … I think perhaps I can, Bob.

McCRAW: Then you'd better (*START FADE*) meet me at King's Cross at about two-fifteen otherwise we might have a little difficulty in …

FADE VOICE.

FADE SCENE and cross to the arrival of a train at a small railway station.

Carriage doors are opened and closed.

McCRAW: (*Pleasantly surprised*) Why, hello, Colonel! How are ye?

SANDOWN: (*Well spoken: about fifty-five*) Ah, hello, Inspector! Nice to see you again! Had a pleasant journey?

McCRAW: Not so bad, laddie, but … why man, you're looking better!

SANDOWN: Think so …?

McCRAW: Good gracious me, yes! … Ye look like a different man! (*Suddenly*) Oh, I'm sorry – d'ye know Mr Starr? Michael Starr – Colonel Sandown.

STARR: How do you do, sir?

SANDOWN: Delighted to meet you, sir! Heard a great deal about you from the Inspector here! Where are you staying, McCraw? The White Horse?

McCRAW: Aye!

SANDOWN: Well, I've got the car outside – no objection if I do a spot of shopping in the village, before I drop you?

McCRAW: No. No, of course not. As a matter of fact Mr Starr here would rather like to send a telegram.

STARR: I was just wondering if the station master could help me – it's rather important.

SANDOWN: Certainly! Ah – here he is!

EDWARDS: (*A wizened little man of about seventy odd: rather a squeaky voice*) Good afternoon, sir! Good afternoon gentlemen!

SANDOWN: Edwards, this gentleman would rather like to use your telephone …

EDWARDS: Certainly, sir … this way, sir.

McCRAW: We'll meet you at the car, Mike.

STARR: Yes, all right, old boy!

SANDOWN: (*Walking away*) It's in the front … You go down to the bottom of the platform and turn left.

STARR: I'll find it …

Pause.

MICHAEL STARR and EDWARDS are walking along the platform.

STARR: You seem to be having a pretty quiet time down here. Is it always like this?

EDWARDS: Always quiet on a Wednesday, it's half day. Mind you – not that we go in for hustle much in these parts – or bustle for that matter!

STARR laughs.

STARR: (*Making conversation*) Well, you've got quite a nice little station.

EDWARDS: Be better when we get a place for folk to sit down in.

STARR: What sort of a village is Redford?

200

EDWARDS: (*Surprised*) Redford? Haven't ye been here a'fore?

STARR: No. I'm afraid not.

EDWARDS: A foreigner?

STARR: Yes, I – er – suppose so …

EDWARDS: M'm – well, there's nothin' the matter with Redford! Nothin' at all! (*Suddenly*) Ah, here's the office! You'll find the telephone on the wall, and if (*START FADE*) you take my tip you'll ask for the supervisor straight away otherwise …

FADE VOICE.

FADE UP the sound of a motor car: it is standing still and in the background.

SANDOWN: Ah! Here's Mr Starr!

McCRAW: Aye – that's Mike!

SANDOWN: You haven't been long, sir!

STARR: I took the short cut through the waiting room.

SANDOWN: Ah yes! Are we ready?

McCRAW: (*Brightly*) It rather looks as if our journey down here was unnecessary, Mike.

STARR: What do you mean?

McCRAW: Apparently the local police made an arrest this morning – they think it's the man we're looking for.

STARR: (*Curtly*) Then I should tell them to think again!

McCRAW: What d'you mean, Mike?

STARR: They've arrested the wrong man!!

McCRAW: What!!

SANDOWN: Why good gracious me, sir, you're not going to infer that …

FADE UP of music.

FADE DOWN.

ANNOUNCER: Who does Michael Starr suspect? Do you know? Later on in the programme you will hear from Michael Starr himself the solution to tonight's detective problem.

Turn over for the solution to mystery twenty-one.

MYSTERY TWENTY-ONE – THE SOLUTION

ANNOUNCER: We now return you to Michael Starr for the solution to tonight's detective problem.

STARR: They've arrested the wrong man!!

MCCRAW: What!!

SANDOWN: Why good gracious me, sir, you're not going to infer that ...

McCRAW: (*Interrupting SANDOWN*) What – what the devil d'you mean, Mike?

STARR: Bob, listen! You told me that the man you were looking for had a secret hideout, otherwise you would have found him. But supposing he hadn't a hideout but was simply a master at disguise?

SANDOWN: What – what are you suggesting?

STARR: I'm suggesting that when Foster came down here someone met him; someone who Foster thought he recognised.

SANDOWN: What – what the devil are you getting at, sir?

STARR: I'm getting at the fact that you are not Colonel Sandown but are in fact the man we're looking for!!

McCRAW: Why, Mike, of course this is the Colonel, I ... I ... (*He hesitates*) I ... I – er ...

STARR: You're not so sure now, are you, Robert? Do you remember what you said when you first saw him? You said, "Why, you look like a different man" ...

McCRAW: Why, yes, but ...

STARR: And there's another point too. I'm sure Colonel Sandown – the real Colonel

	Sandown – would hardly have suggested ... shopping ... in ... the village.
SANDOWN:	(*Tensely*) Why not?
STARR:	Because today happens to be early closing day, my friend! And there's another point too, while we're talking about it. For a so-called native of these parts you don't seem to be very well acquainted with the railway station here, do you?
SANDOWN:	What – what do you mean?
STARR:	I mean, my friend, that I could hardly have taken a short cut through the waiting room since there doesn't happen to be a waiting room!!
SANDOWN:	Why, you ...
McCRAW:	Look out!!!
STARR:	Don't let him get in the car, Bob, or ...
STARR strikes out. We hear a thud as SANDOWN falls.	
McCRAW:	Oh, nice work, Mike! You've knocked him cold!
STARR:	Search him, Bob!
McCRAW:	O.K. (*A moment's pause*) Oh! Oh! Here's a nice peaceful looking weapon!
STARR:	We'll dump him in the car!
McCRAW:	I say, what – what the Dickens was he going to do with us?
STARR:	He was going to do precisely the same with us that he did with Foster. Take us for a ride and then ...
McCRAW:	And then ... the ... river?
STARR:	Exactly! Come on, Bob – we'll take him down to the police station. I'm sure your friend Colonel Sandown will be highly amused when he ...

FADE UP of music.

MYSTERY TWENTY-TWO

Cast:

Michael Starr	Henry Oscar
Inspector McCraw	Ian Sadler
Dale Morgan	Frank Cochran
Trevor Davies	Basil Jones
Mr Spearman	Cyril Gardiner

As the opening music finishes CROSS FADE to an open air scene on a golf course.

MICHAEL STARR and INSPECTOR McCRAW are playing golf.

McCRAW: Now keep your head down, laddie! And keep your eye on the ball. Now take the club back slowly ... Slowly, Mike! ...

STARR: (*Amused, yet faintly irritated*) I say, just a minute, old boy – I've been playing this game for twelve years.

McCRAW: I know, Mike, but it's never too late to learn!

STARR: (*Aghast*) Why – why – why good heavens, Bob, I'm already five up and there's only another ...

McCRAW: Now, Mike! Now ye know perfectly well that if I hadn't got into that confounded bunker I'd have been ...

STARR: Pardon me for asking, old boy – but which bunker do you mean? The one in which you took fifteen or the one in which you took fourteen?

McCRAW: (*Shocked*) Why, Mike! Mike, as long as I ...

In the background a shot is heard.

McCRAW: ... live and breathe I swear that I only took ...

STARR: (*Quietly: interrupting McCRAW*) I say ... did you hear that?

McCRAW: What?

STARR: That shot.

McCRAW: Yes, it's old man Spearman shooting rabbits. He's always shooting 'em. (*Impatiently*) Now what was I saying, laddie? Oh, yes! Yes, about that bunker! As long as I ... (*Suddenly*) What the devil's that?

A pause.

209

In the distant background DALE MORGAN can be heard shouting: "Help! Help! Help! etc etc."

STARR: There's someone shouting for help!

The shouting continues.

McCRAW: He's over on the other side ... on the first.

STARR: Come along, Bob!!

McCRAW: (*Starting to hurry*) I wonder what the devil's the matter? Surely it can't be anything to do with that shot we heard or we should have ...

STARR: (*Suddenly*) There he is!

McCRAW: Why – why – it's Dale Morgan!

STARR: Do you know him?

McCRAW: He's a Canadian. Only been a member here about ... I say, the laddie looks pretty excited!!

STARR: There's someone else, Bob, and ... Look!! ... on the tee!

McCRAW: Mike, there's been an accident or ... something.

STARR: Yes, yes, looks very much like it.

McCRAW: If we take a short cut (*START FADE*) across this green it'll bring us to the bottom of the first fairway and then we can cut across the ...

FADE SCENE.

CROSS FADE to DALE MORGAN. He is a Canadian: about forty-five. At the moment he is faintly confused.

MORGAN: Say I ... I don't know what the hell happened ... I kinda heard Mr Spearman here taking a pot shot at the rabbits and the next thing I knew was that poor John here was ... flat on his face ...

McCRAW: Is – is he dead, Mike?

STARR: Yes.

MORGAN: (*Stunned*) Dead! Good God, don't – don't say he's – he's dead?!

SPEARMAN: (*An old man: essentially of the country*) Why – why – this is terrible! Terrible! He can't be dead, why …

STARR: Mr Spearman, what sort of a gun are you using?

SPEARMAN: Why – why a sporting rifle, sir, a twenty-two bore.

STARR: And not shot cartridges, I see – but bullets. M'm.

SPEARMAN: But, Mr Starr, I – I couldn't have shot Mr Dent – not from where I be standing … Why – why I be right over on the other side o' the fence.

McCRAW: Well, I'm afraid it looks rather as if ye did, laddie. O' course accidents will happen in the best o' …

SPEARMAN: But – but this is terrible! Nothing's ever happened to me like this before! Why I be … Are you sure he's dead? Can't we get a doctor, and …

STARR: I'm afraid not, Mr Spearman.

McCRAW: (*Softly*) It's too late for a doctor, laddie.

STARR: Mr Morgan, supposing you tell us – what … happened … exactly …

MORGAN: Well, now … John … Mr Dent here … was just going to take his drive – you can see he's got his driver in his hand – when suddenly we heard a shot. Almost simultaneously John fell forward on his face. I thought at first he was joking, but … well … when I saw the blood I knew then that it was … it was no joke.

STARR: And you, Mr Spearman?

SPEARMAN: I – I don't know what … what to say. You see … I – I was over on the far side o' that fence. I saw a rabbit and … simply took aim … the next thing I know was that I – I heard Mr Morgan … shouting for help.

STARR: You were surprised when he told you that you'd accidentally hit Mr Dent?

SPEARMAN: But of course I be surprised. I be shooting across that hedge towards the copse.

STARR: I see. (*Suddenly*) Did you … er … know Mr Dent, by any chance?

SPEARMAN: Er – yes. Yes, he … he was once very kind to me. About two years ago I was in pretty low water and Mr Dent, well, he …

MORGAN: (*Pleasantly*) He lent you two hundred pounds.

SPEARMAN: (*Surprised*) Why, yes! Did – did Mr Dent tell you that?

MORGAN: (*With a laugh*) Sure, he did! That two hundred didn't come out of his picket, you know. It came out of the firm.

STARR: I take it, Mr Morgan, that you were in partnership with Mr Dent?

MORGAN: Yes, we have a machine-tool business.

STARR: I see. Thank you … (*Briskly*) Come along, Bob – you'd better telephone the local people.

McCRAW: Aye!

SPEARMAN: Have we to wait here or …

STARR: Yes, we shan't keep you long …

MORGAN: Sure is a most unfortunate business …

SPEARMAN: But what I can't understand, Mr Morgan, is (*START FADE*) if I be firing towards that copse then how on earth did I manage to …

FADE SCENE.

FADE UP of TREVOR DAVIES. He is a typical, faintly exciteable, Welshman of about forty.

TREVOR: I can hardly believe it, it seems such a remarkable thing to happen. And right under our very noses as you might say. Why I've been the Pro here for ten years and I've never yet heard of a case where ...

STARR: (*Interrupting TREVOR on the word 'heard'*) Mr Davies, tell me – did Mr Dent play a great deal of golf?

TREVOR: Oh, yes, he was a splendid golfer. Of course he used to drive with his iron and was a little shady on his putting perhaps, but ... (*With a little laugh*) ... aren't we all?

STARR: What about Mr Morgan?

TREVOR: The Canadian gentleman? I – I ... don't know a great deal about Mr Morgan. He's only just started to play golf, you know. Must say I was surprised to see him playing with Mr Dent.

STARR: Why?

TREVOR: Well – I don't want to tell stories out of school – but ... (*He hesitates*) ... but they do say that Mr Morgan and Mr Dent did not get on well together. Mr Morgan, they say, was trying to get control of the business. He's a nice man is Mr Morgan, but ... Ah! Here's the Inspector!

McCRAW: Afternoon, Trevor!

TREVOR: Good afternoon, Inspector – what a distressing business this is, to be sure.

McCRAW: Yes – yes, most unfortunate.

STARR: (*Dismissing him*) Thank you, sir – you've been a great help.

TREVOR:	Only too happy to have been of service, Mr Starr. Good afternoon, sir! Good afternoon, Inspector!
McCRAW:	Goodbye, Trevor.
TREVOR:	(*To himself: walking away*) Most distressing business ... most distressing ...
STARR:	(*Crisply*) Well?
McCRAW:	(*Excitedly: yes rather mystified*) I did exactly what ye told me, Mike! I went into the field and I walked across from where ...
STARR:	From where Spearman stood and fired his shot ... to the copse ... Well????
McCRAW:	Well – I – I found a rabbit, Mike!! A dead rabbit! It – it had been shot!
STARR:	That's just what I suspected ...
McCRAW:	But – but, Mike, if Spearman hit the rabbit, how on earth ...
STARR:	How ... on earth could he have ... killed ... Mr Dent? Exactly!!!!

FADE UP of music.
FADE DOWN.

ANNOUNCER:	Later in the programme you will hear from Michael Starr himself the solution to tonight's detective problem.

214

Turn over to find the solution to mystery twenty-two.

MYSTERY TWENTY-TWO – THE SOLUTION

ANNOUNCER: We now return you to Michael Starr for the solution to tonight's detective problem.

McCRAW: But – but, Mike, if Spearman hit the rabbit, how on earth …

STARR: How … on earth could he have … killed … Mr Dent? Exactly!!!!

McCRAW: Mike!! Mike, what the devil are ye getting at?

STARR: I'm getting at the fact that Spearman didn't kill Dent!

McCRAW: What! (*Tensely*) Then who did?

STARR: Dale Morgan!

McCRAW: Morgan!

STARR: In my opinion Dent was shot at close quarters and shot before he arrived at the golf links. Morgan brought him here and dumped him on the first tee. He knew that Spearman was shooting rabbits in the adjoining field and once Spearman made a shot in the right direction – or what sounded like the right direction – Morgan raised the alarm.

McCRAW: But supposing someone had seen Morgan carrying Dent down to the tee?

STARR: He had to take that chance. After all, the course is always pretty deserted during the week, isn't it?

McCRAW: Yes, but – what about a motive?

STARR: You ask Trevor about the motive. Apparently it's common gossip that

	Morgan's been trying to get control of the business.

McCRAW: But – But it doesn't make sense, laddie! Why – why Morgan and Dent were just about to play a round of golf. Dent was practically about to drive – he had the driver actually in his hand!

STARR: Yes! Exactly!

McCRAW: What – what do you mean?

STARR: I mean, my dear Robert, that Dent never used a driver, he always drove with an iron!!!

McCRAW: Well, I'll be … Mike! Mike, why the devil didn't I notice that!!

STARR: (*Magnanimously*) Oh, don't let that worry you, old boy! After all, it's never too late to learn …

FADE UP of music.

MYSTERY TWENTY-THREE

Cast:

Michael Starr . . . . Henry Oscar
Inspector McCraw . . . . Ian Sadler
Lucy Davenport . . . . .Belle Chrystall
Tom Davenport . . . . .Peter Cousins

As the opening music finishes CROSS FADE to INSPECTOR McCRAW.

McCRAW: Well, there they are, Mike! That's all we've got to work on! Exhibit A! Exhibit B! Exhibit C! Well, laddie, what do ye make of 'em?

STARR: (*Glibly*) Well, I should say Exhibit A looks like a dagger, Exhibit B looks like a wristlet watch and Exhibit C looks remarkably like a book.

McCRAW: (*Exasperated*) Dammit, laddie, I know that! But what do you make of 'em?

STARR: (*Amused*) What do you expect me to make of them?

McCRAW: (*Still faintly exasperated*) Well, I suppose you've heard of Mrs Hodder?

STARR: Mrs Joshua Hodder?

McCRAW: Aye!

STARR: Yes, I've heard of her, of course. Now let me see! (*Thoughtfully*) Lives in St John's Wood. Reputed to be worth three quarters of a million. Once wrote a book called The Gentle Art of Listening.

McCRAW: Aye, that's right.

STARR: (*Curious*) Bob, why are you so interested in Mrs Hodder?

McCRAW: She's dead. She was murdered, Mike.

STARR: When?

McCRAW: Last night at about a quarter past eight.

STARR: Go on, Bob.

McCRAW: At about nine o'clock I had a telephone call. It was from a Miss Davenport.

STARR: And who, precisely, is Miss Davenport?

McCRAW: She's Mrs Hodder's niece. Both she and her brother Tom have been living with Mrs Hodder for the past four years. Anyway, to cut a long story short, the niece went into the lounge at about five minutes to nine. She found Mrs Hodder on the floor and the room in more or less a complete shambles. She also found this dagger – it was in a corner of the room and was covered in blood.

STARR: Mrs Hodder, I take it, had been stabbed?

McCRAW: I should say so, laddie! According to the police surgeon the wound was at least four inches deep.

STARR: M'm. Did Miss Davenport recognise the dagger?

McCRAW: She says she's never seen it before – but I fancy she's lying. Rather gave me the impression that it belongs to her brother.

STARR: What about a motive?

McCRAW: Well, I suppose the only person with a motive is Miss Davenport. She inherits the family fortune. But she certainly didn't commit the murder.

STARR: How do you know?

McCRAW: Because the murder was committed at a quarter past eight and at eight-fifteen Miss Davenport was in the public library.

STARR: Did anyone see her there?

McCRAW: Yes, the librarian, and ... oh, dozens of people.

STARR: How do you know the murder was committed at a quarter past eight?

MccRAW: By the wristlet watch! Take a look at it, Mike! It was obviously smashed during the course of the struggle and it obviously says ...

STARR: It obviously says – a quarter past eight. Yes, a little too obviously for my liking! Let me have a look at that book, Bob.

McCRAW:	We found it on the floor near the body.
STARR:	(*Examining the book*) M'm – A Tale of Two Cities by Charles Dickens. Pages four and five uncut, pages seven and (*Suddenly: surprised*) I say, this looks to me like a first edition!
McCRAW:	Aye, the old lady had rather a fine collection of books, Mike.
STARR:	M'm. (*Suddenly*) Robert, tell me: how does Miss Davenport get on with her brother?
McCRAW:	Not very well, I'm afraid. You see, Miss Davenport was a great favourite with the old lady and Tom sort of – well – rather resented it. He's a peculiar sort of bird! Terribly – er – supercilious.
STARR:	I'd rather like a word with him – and Miss Davenport too for that matter.
McCRAW:	Then come on, laddie, we'll go along to the house.
STARR:	Oh, er – by the way …
McCRAW:	Yes, Mike?
STARR:	How long was Tom Davenport out in South Africa?
McCRAW:	South Africa! (*Surprised*) Has he been to South Africa?
STARR:	Yes. Yes, I think so, Bob.
McCRAW:	Mike … But how do you know?
STARR:	That knife …
McCRAW:	What about the knife?
STARR:	Well, in the first place, I shall be very surprised if it doesn't belong to Tom Davenport and secondly I'm pretty certain it comes from South Africa.
McCRAW:	(*Bewildered*) But he says he's never seen the knife before!

223

STARR: Of course he does! (*Laughing*) Come along, Bob – I've got my car outside.

McCRAW: (*START FADE*) Mike, there are times when I find ye so exasperating that I swear I'll never …

FADE SCENE.

FADE UP of LUCY DAVENPORT.

LUCY: Mr Starr, surely you're not going to go all over this dreadful …

STARR: (*Interrupting LUCY*) Now, Miss Davenport, please! I should just like to verify the facts, if you don't mind! You say that immediately after tea Mrs Hodder and yourself went into the lounge?

LUCY: Yes. Mrs Hodder started to read A Tale of Two Cities. It was a book which, oddly enough, neither of us had read before so she offered to read it aloud to me. Mrs Hodder was very fond of reading aloud, you know.

TOM: She certainly was! Never knew an old lady so fond of her own voice!

LUCY: Tom, please! (*After a moment*) Mrs Hodder was a delightful reader, Mr Starr, she had a lovely voice and she made every character seem – well – almost alive.

STARR: What time did Mrs Hodder start to read the book?

LUCY: Let me see … It would be about … Oh, I should say about six o'clock.

STARR: And she finished reading at about …?

LUCY: At about half past seven.

STARR: It take it that – er – shortly after that you went out to the library?

LUCY:	Yes.
STARR:	Thank you.
TOM:	(*With sarcasm*) Now it's my turn, eh, Mr Starr?
STARR:	Yes, Mr Davenport. Now it's your turn.
TOM:	(*With heavy sarcasm*) And where were you at the time of the murder, my man?
STARR:	(*Calmly: unruffled*) Yes, Mr Davenport – if it comes to that – where were you at the time of the murder?
TOM:	I'm afraid I've got a particularly weak alibi, Mr Starr. After tea I went to my room – which is on the second floor – and stayed there until … until Lucy told me about … about the murder.
McCRAW:	Did ye hear your sister go out to the library?
TOM:	I never heard anything, Inspector. I was extremely busy. I'm – I'm writing a novel.
McCRAW:	M'm. Tell me: have you ever been to South Africa, Mr Davenport?
LUCY:	Yes. He was there for two years in the consular service.
STARR:	Thank you, Miss Davenport. That's all we wanted to know. Come along, Robert. Let's go back to Scotland Yard. (*START FADE*) It's all right, I think we can find our way out of the house …

FADE SCENE.

FADE UP of McCRAW.

McCRAW:	Mike, I'm bewildered! I'm confused! I'm – why man, if it wasn't for me strong …
STARR:	Take it easy, laddie! Take it easy! (*Calmly*) Now, in the first place, Bob, you see that dagger …
McCRAW:	Aye!

STARR:	Well – measure the blade …
McCRAW:	What?
STARR:	Measure the blade …
McCRAW:	(*After a moment*) Why – why it's only two and a half inches …
STARR:	Exactly!
McCRAW:	Why – why the knife couldn't have killed Mrs Hodder!
STARR:	Exactly!
McCRAW:	(*Seriously*) Mike, do you know who killed the old lady?
STARR:	Yes. Yes … I … know … Bob.

FADE UP of music.

FADE DOWN.

ANNOUNCER: Do you know who murdered Mrs Hodder? Later in the programme you will hear from Michael Starr himself the solution to tonight's detective problem.

Turn over the page to find the solution to mystery twenty-three.

ANNOUNCER: We now return you to Michael Starr for the solution to tonight's detective problem.

McCRAW: (*Seriously*) Mike, do you know who killed the old lady?

STARR: Yes. Yes ... I ... know ... Bob.

McCRAW: Then for heaven's sake, laddie, please ...

STARR: Listen! And listen very carefully! It was obvious from the beginning that either Miss Davenport had committed the murder and planted the knife in order to throw suspicion onto her brother, or Tom had committed the murder and planted the knife in order to throw suspicion onto his sister. Now when you spoke to Miss Davenport about the knife ...

McCRAW: She gave us a pretty broad hint that it belonged to her brother.

STARR: Exactly!

McCRAW: But Miss Davenport couldn't have committed the murder – she has a foolrpoof alibi.

STARR: Providing the murder was committed at a quarter past eight.

McCRAW: But wasn't it committed at a quarter past eight?

STARR: No! After tea, Tom went upstairs to his room and Miss Davenport and Mrs Hodder went into the lounge. It was THEN that Miss Davenport committed the murder, altered the watch to a quarter past eight, and substituted her brother's knife for the one

	with which she murdered the old lady. But Miss Davenport made one fatal mistake! She took a novel from the bookcase and dropped it by the body. Later she told us that Mrs Hodder had been reading from the book for an hour and a half.
McCRAW:	What are ye getting at, Mike?
STARR:	Mrs Hodder never read from this book for an hour and a half, laddie! Pages four and five are still uncut! When you're reading a novel for the first time you don't usually skip two pages, do you, Robert?
McCRAW:	(*Astonished*) Well, I … Mike, this has certainly been some case.
STARR:	Yes. I think one might almost say a Dickens of a case, eh, old boy? (*He chuckles*)

FADE UP of music.

Sadly the script of Mystery Twenty-four no longer survives in the archive.

MYSTERY TWENTY-FIVE

Cast:

Michael Starr . . . . Henry Oscar

Inspector McCraw . . . . Ian Sadler

Mr Terence . . . . Harry Hutchinson

Daly . . . . .Preston Lockwood

Eldridge . . . . .Fred Yule

Mabel . . . . Freda Falconer

As the opening music finishes CROSS FADE to the voice of DAN TERENCE who is a middle-aged Irishman.

TERENCE: (*Flustered*) Inspector … Mr Starr … I'm mighty sorry to be interrupting your game of snooker but t'is a spot of bother we're having in the Club bar.

McCRAW: What is it, Mr Terence?

TERENCE: Well, sir, it's Mr Daly, sir …

STARR: What about Mr Daly?

TERENCE: He – He appears to have been poisoned, sir.

McCRAW: (*Astonished*) Poisoned?!

TERENCE: Yes, sir.

STARR: Poisoned – what with?

TERENCE: With the beer, sir.

McCRAW: (*Faintly amused*) Well, I've told ye! I've been complaining about the beer for some time, laddie! Come along, Mike! (*START FADE*) We'd better look into this little matter just in case there has been any …

FADE SCENE.

FADE UP of two or three voices in animated conversation: there is a sudden silence.

McCRAW: (*Tensely*) Well, Mike?

STARR: (*Quietly*) He's dead …

TERENCE: Dead! Dead … did you say? But man, he can't be dead, why … that's impossible!

STARR: Is this the tankard he was drinking out of?

TERENCE: I'm – I'm not sure. Is that his tankard, Mr Eldridge?

ELDRIDGE: (*Rather a well spoken man of about sixty odd*) Yes … Yes, that's his tankard …

STARR: M'm …

233

ELDRIDGE: Terence, this is dreadful, I – I can hardly believe it, why …

STARR: Do you mind if I use your office, Mr Terence? I'd rather like to have a chat with the Inspector.

TERENCE: Go ahead, sir! Go ahead!

STARR: Thank you.

McCRAW: I'll be with ye in a minute, Mike – (*START FADE*) I just want to have a word with Mr Terence here about the circumstances leading up to the …

FADE SCENE.

FADE UP of INSPECTOR McCRAW.

McCRAW: Mike! Mike, what the devil are ye trying to tell me?

STARR: I'm trying to tell you, my dear Robert, that this case is quite unquestionably a case of … murder!

McCRAW: What!

STARR: Daly was poisoned. He was poisoned with arsenic.

McCRAW: Are you sure, laddie?

STARR: Positive! Now come on, Bob – give me the details. What did Terence tell you?

McCRAW: Well … it appears that Daly was sort of unofficially engaged to David Eldridge's daughter. Eldridge wasn't at all keen on the idea, although according to Terence he appeared to keep on quite friendly terms with Daly, I rather think he quite liked Daly as a friend, but …

STARR: But he didn't fancy him as a son-in-law?

McCRAW: That's about it!

STARR: (*After a moment*) What … exactly … happened … tonight?

McCRAW: (*Thoughtfully*) I don't know. But I rather feel that there must have been some sort of a row. Mabel says that …

STARR: Mabel? Who's Mabel?

McCRAW: She's the girl behind the bar. The one that served the drinks.

STARR: (*Crisply*) Get her in here. I'd like to talk to her!

McCRAW: Well, as a matter of fact, I told the lassie to report here as soon …

The door opens.

McCRAW: … Ah, come in, Mabel!

MABEL: (*Chirpy, cockney, but rather likeable*) Hope I haven't kept you waiting! I know what you gentlemen are! (*Suddenly*) Hello! Are you the Michael Starr I've heard so much about?

STARR: That's right.

MABEL: (*Cheekily*) I like the look of you, I must say.

STARR: I must say, I like the look of you, too, Mabel.

McCRAW: (*Clearing his throat*) Yes, well – er –

STARR: (*Seriously*) Mabel, I want you to tell me exactly what happened from the moment Mr Daly came into the bar.

MABEL: Well, it would be about a quarter past eight. I was cleaning some glasses and doing a bit o' tidying up when (*SLOW FADE*) suddenly the door opened and Mr Daly and Mr Eldridge popped in. Mr Daly looked rather annoyed I thought, and I distinctly remember hearing him say to Mr Eldridge …

FADE.

CROSS FADE into the next scene.

235

DALY:	(*A self-possessed man: at the moment faintly annoyed*) All right, Eldridge, there's – there's no need to say anything more about the matter!
ELDRIDGE:	My dear Carl, don't be stupid! Remember you're a man of the world and stop behaving like a lovesick schoolboy! (*Pleasantly*) Now what are you going to have to drink?
DALY:	Er – Oh … half of mild …
ELDRIDGE:	Two halves, Mabel.
MABEL:	Ta.
DALY:	Have you got a match?
ELDRIDGE:	'Fraid I haven't …
MABEL:	There's a box over there – on the mantelpiece.
DALY:	Oh, thanks.
A pause.	
ELDRIDGE:	Keep the change, Mabel.
MABEL:	Ta.
ELDRIDGE:	(*Raising his voice*) Here's your drink … (*Aside*) All the best, Mabel! (*He drinks*)
A pause.	
DALY:	(*At the bar again*) Won't you have a drink, Mabel?
MABEL:	Ya. Don't mind if I do, Mr Daly. (*Suddenly*) Good evening, Mr Terence!
TERENCE:	Evening! Good evening, gentlemen!
ELDRIDGE:	Hello, Terence! What are you going to have?
TERENCE:	Well now, I'll have a little …
DALY:	(*Interrupting TERENCE: quietly*) I say, Eldridge – have you had a drink out of this?
ELDRIDGE:	Don't be silly, old man – that's your tankard.
DALY:	Yes, but I think you must have had a drink out of it by mistake because I haven't touched it yet and it … (*Suddenly*) I say, what's the matter?

ELDRIDGE: It's – it's my stomach, I ... I ... God, I do feel awful!

TERENCE: You'd better sit down, man!

ELDRIDGE: Have you – Have you got any milk of magnesia, Terence?

TERENCE: Yes, there's some in the office – I'll fetch it if you like.

DALY: You certainly look off colour! (*He laughs*) Your very good health! (*He drinks. He gives a sudden gasp and drops the tankard*)

MABEL screams.

MABEL: Mr Terence!!! Look!!! Look at Mr Daly!!

ELDRIDGE: What – What's the matter with him?

TERENCE: My God, he looks as if ... he's ... been poisoned ...

ELDRIDGE: Poisoned!!

TERENCE: Yes. Are you all right, Eldridge?

ELDRIDGE: Yes! But don't bother about me! Get a doctor!

TERENCE: (*Flustered*) Er – telephone for a doctor, Mabel! I'll – I'll – I'll fetch Inspector McCraw. (*START FADE*) He's in the billiard room so he might just as well have a look at ...

FADE SCENE.

CROSS FADE back to the voice of MABEL.

MABEL: ... and then of course shortly after that you and the Inspector turned up.

STARR: And you were telephoning?

MABEL: Yes, that's right.

STARR: Has the doctor arrived?

MABEL: Yes, I think he's just come.

STARR: Well, thank you, Mabel, you've been a great help.

MABEL: Yes, well ... I like to please!

STARR: Well, you've certainly pleased me, Mabel.
                In fact, you've told me who murdered …
                Mr Daly …
McCRAW: WHAT!!!
FADE UP of music.

FADE DOWN.

ANNOUNCER: Do you know who murdered Carl Daly?
                Later in the programme you will hear from
                Michael Starr himself the solution to
                tonight's detective problem.

Turn over for the solution to mystery twenty-five.

ANNOUNCER: We now return you to Michael Starr for the solution to tonight's detective problem.

STARR: Well, you've certainly pleased me, Mabel. In fact, you've told me who murdered ... Mr Daly ...

McCRAW: WHAT!!!

MABEL: Was – Was Mr Daly ... murdered ...?

STARR: He was ... by ... David Eldridge. You see, Eldridge dropped the poison into Daly's tankard whilst ...

McCRAW: Whilst Daly was getting the box of matches from the mantelpiece!

STARR: Exactly! But do you remember what Mabel told us, Bob? She said that for a moment Daly laboured under the impression that Eldridge had, by mistake, taken a drink from his tankard – the tankard containing the poison. Eldridge became confused: he wasn't sure whether he had or he hadn't. He became frightened, nervous, imagined himself in pain, and then ... (*Slowly*) ... and then when he saw the real effect of the poison – in other words when Daly took it – he knew then that ...

McCRAW: ... that he hadn't taken any personally!

STARR: Exactly!

McCRAW: But, Mike, how can you prove this?

STARR: When Eldridge thought that, by accident, he'd poisoned himself he sent the

	Secretary, Mr Terence, for some milk of magnesia.
McCRAW:	Well?
STARR:	Well, by doing that he openly admitted that he knew that if he had been poisoned he'd been poisoned with ARSENIC!
McCRAW:	How the devil do ye make that out?
STARR:	Well, you see Robert, milk of magnesia happens to be a rough antidote for arsenic poisoning!
McCRAW:	Well, I'll be … Mike, you're a genius! You're a wizard! You're …
MABEL:	Oh, Mr Starr, I think you're wonderful!
STARR:	I think you're wonderful too, Mabel!
MABEL:	(*Coyly*) You – you are only pulling my leg now.
STARR:	(*Imitating MABEL*) Not in front of the Inspector, Mabel!

FADE UP of music.

MYSTERY TWENTY-SIX
Cast:

Michael Starr . . . . Henry Oscar
Inspector McCraw . . . . Ian Sadler
Davidson . . . . Lewis Stringer
Ward . . . . .Eric Clavering

As the opening music finishes CROSS FADE to INSPECTOR McCRAW.

McCRAW: (*Extremely angry*) Mike, it's the most bewildering, confusing, irritating, exasperating case I've ever heard of! Why man, if it wasn't for m'a strong constitution I'd ...

STARR: (*Interrupting McCRAW*) You wouldn't know what to talk about! But never mind your constitution, Robert, let's have the details.

McCRAW: But, man, there aren't any details – that's what makes it so exasperating!

STARR: You seem to forget, Bob – you haven't told me yet ... what ... happened?

McCRAW: About six months ago a jeweller – chappie by the name of Ricentio – arrived in this country from South America. He had a necklace – a diamond necklace valued at approximately a quarter of a million. Six weeks after Ricentio arrived another gentleman landed – a notorious crook by the name of Joe Sutton. The F.B.I. warned us about Sutton but he slipped through our fingers. You see, laddie, Sutton intended to ... get ... the necklace ...

STARR: Well?

McCRAW: Last night Ricentio was murdered and the necklace disappeared.

STARR: (*After a low whistle of surprise*) What's Sutton like?

McCRAW: We don't know. We've never seen him. He's an American, that's all we know.

STARR: M'm. Where did Ricentio live?

McCRAW: In a block of flats just off Park Lane. The janitor found the body at about a quarter past

	six this morning. He dashed out of the flat and bumped straight into one of our new fellows – plain clothes laddie name o' Davidson. Would you like a word with Davidson – he's in the next office?
STARR:	Yes. Yes, I would. (*After a moment*) How old was Ricentio?
McCRAW:	Oh, about fifty-two or three.
STARR:	Have you any details about Sutton? What did the F.B.I. send you?
McCRAW:	They told us that he was a comparatively young man and that he was as slippery as an eel. They also said that he could disguise both his voice and his appearance. He was born in New York.
STARR:	M'm.

A door opens.

DAVIDSON:	(*With a faint cockney accent*) Did you want me, sir?
McCRAW:	Aye! Come in, Davidson! This is Mr Michael Starr.
DAVIDSON:	Oh, how do you do, sir?
STARR:	What happened last night – or rather this morning – Davidson?
DAVIDSON:	Well, I was passing down Park Lane, sir, when one o' the janitors suddenly popped out o' one o' the big buildings an' dashed across the sidewalk. He was in a proper tear, I can tell you. Anyhow, after I calmed him down a bit, I got a bit o' sense out of the lad. He said there'd been a murder – I went back into the building with him and we took the elevator to an apartment on the fourth floor.
STARR:	And you found Ricentio?

DAVIDSON:	Yes, sir. The room was in a terrible mess – and the safe was off its hinges.
STARR:	Did you see anyone else in the building besides the janitor?
DAVIDSON:	Yes, sir. Just as I was leaving I bumped into a Mr Ward – he's a Canadian gentleman with an apartment on the fifth floor. He was just coming back from a party.
McCRAW:	At a quarter past six!
STARR:	Did you tell him about the murder?
DAVIDSON:	No, sir. I simply told him that I was a police officer and I asked him to account for his movements.
STARR:	How did he impress you?
DAVIDSON:	Not very well, sir. For one thing I don't think he's a Canadian. I've never been to America, sir, but I'd like to bet Mr Ward's an American gentleman.
STARR:	Have you checked up on Ward?
McCRAW:	Yes. He's a Canadian all right – born in Ontario.
DAVIDSON:	I took the liberty of asking Mr Ward to call at the Yard, sir. He's waiting in the Superintendent's office.
STARR:	Good idea, Davidson! Come along, Bob! I'd like a word with this young man.
DAVIDSON:	Oh, he's not very (*START FADE*) young, sir. I should say he's at least five or six years older than the Inspector, although of course it's always rather difficult to judge the …

FADE SCENE.

CROSS FADE to the voice of SAM WARD. He is a Canadian.

WARD:	… Say, you seem to be asking me an awful lot of questions, Mr Starr!
STARR:	I've got rather a curious disposition!
WARD:	Yeah – well suppose you try and satisfy my curiosity for a change. What exactly happened last night in Castleford Mansions?
McCRAW:	You tell him, Davidson.
DAVIDSON:	Mr Ricentio was murdered, sir.
WARD:	Ricentio? Why – why, he's the jeweller! He lives just below me on the fourth floor.
STARR:	That's right.
WARD:	(*Astonished*) Ricentio? Well – what do you know about this? Why – why I only saw the guy yesterday morning. He seemed quite cheerful.
STARR:	Mr Ward, tell me – is that your real name – Victor Edward Ward?
WARD:	Why of course it is!
STARR:	And you've been in this country since October 21st, 1936?
WARD:	That's right!
STARR:	When was the last time you visited America?
WARD:	(*Faintly exasperated*) I tell you I've never been to America! I'm a Canadian – I was born in Ontario.
DAVIDSON:	(*Astonished*) Here – what's this? You say, you've never been to America?
WARD:	Sure I say I've never been to America. There's thousands of Canadians that's never been to America. What's so crazy about that?
DAVIDSON:	But last night – or rather early this morning – you told me that you'd spent six months in Chicago!
WARD:	WHAT!!!

DAVIDSON: Do you deny it?

WARD: Of course I deny it! (*Staggered*) Say, is this guy nuts?

McCRAW: (*Exasperated*) Did ye tell him ye'd spent six months in Chicago or didn't ye?

WARD: Of course I didn't!! I tell you I've never been to the States!!!

STARR: There's no need to get excited, Mr Ward. Let's keep the whole interview on a very friendly basis.

McCRAW: (*Bewildered*) Mike, what the devil are ye grinning at?

STARR: I'm grinning, my dear Robert, because this case is really quite simple. You see, we know that John Sutton murdered Ricentio – so all we've got to do is …

McCRAW: All we've got to do is to find John Sutton!!!!

STARR: Exactly!

McCRAW: (*Sharply*) What d'you mean – Exactly!?

STARR: I mean, my dear Robert, that – er – we've found him.

McCRAW: WHAT!!! You mean to stand there and calmly announce that …

FADE UP of music.
FADE DOWN.

ANNOUNCER: Who does Michael Starr suspect? Do you know? Later in the programme you will hear from Michael Starr himself the solution to tonight's detective problem.

MYSTERY TWENTY-SIX – THE SOLUTION

ANNOUNCER: We now return you to Michael Starr for the solution to tonight's detective problem.

STARR: I mean, my dear Robert, that – er – we've found him.

McCRAW: WHAT!!! You mean to stand there and calmly announce that ...

DAVIDSON: (*Suddenly: tensely*) Stand back!!! Stand back!!! If anybody moves – God help them!!

McCRAW: (*Astonished*) Davidson, why ...

WARD: Put that gun down you crazy young fool, or I'll ...

A shot is fired.

WARD: OW!! (*Weakly*) Oh ... Oh ... my arm!

McCRAW: Why – why, you've shot him!

STARR: You swine I'll ...

DAVIDSON: (*Wildly*) Don't move! Don't move, Starr, or you'll get the same! D'you hear me – don't move!!

McCRAW: (*Bewildered*) Are you ... John Sutton?

DAVIDSON: Of course I'm John Sutton! (*Amused*) You didn't think of looking for me at Scotland Yard, did you, Inspector? Although you guessed who I was, didn't you, Starr?

STARR: (*Quietly*) Yes. Yes, I guessed.

DAVIDSON: What made you suspicious? (*Angry: after a pause*) D'you hear me? What made you suspicious?!!!

STARR: Well, you see, my dear fellow ... (*He makes a move*)

DAVIDSON: (*Quickly*) Oh, no you don't!!! Stand away from that desk or by Jupiter I'll let the daylight into you!! (*After a moment*) Now answer me! What made you suspicious?!!!

STARR: Well, you see, Davidson, I thought it was rather a big coincidence that you happened to be in Park Lane just when the murder was committed, and secondly you seemed quite determined to throw suspicion on to Mr Ward, and thirdly ... (*He hesitates*)

DAVIDSON: Well?

STARR: Thirdly: although you gave an extremely good impersonation of an Englishman I knew for certain that you were an American. You see, you – er – made one or two rather unfortunate slips.

DAVIDSON: What do you mean?

STARR: You referred to the pavement as the sidewalk! You referred to the lift as an elevator! And you referred to Mr Ward's flat as an apartment!

DAVIDSON: (*Angrily*) Why, you clever devil, I'll ...

McCRAW: Look out, Mike!!

A second shot is heard followed by a smashing of glass.

STARR: He's hit the window!

A wild struggle commences.

McCRAW: Oh, nice tackle! Nice tackle! Nice ...

STARR: (*Tensely*) Don't keep on saying "Nice tackle"! Sit on him! Sit on him!!! For heaven's sake, sit on him, Bob!!

McCRAW: (*Completely out of breath*) Man, I – I – I – I – I – I am sitting on him!!

STARR: Why, Robert, you're out of breath!

251

McCRAW: (*Gasping*) Of course I'm out of breath you chump, you don't expect …

STARR: (*Imitating McCRAW*) WHAT! Out of breath! A laddie with your constitution!!! Why, Bob, I'm surprised! Man, I'm surprised!!!

FADE UP closing music.
FADE DOWN.

ANNOUNCER: That was the final programme in the series Michael Starr Investigates.

THE MEMOIRS OF
ANDRE d'ARNELL

A series of nine detective problems, broadcast on the BBC Home
Service from 9 October to 27 November and 18 December 1944 in
the weekly variety show *Monday Night at Eight*, produced by Harry
S. Pepper

MYSTERY ONE

Cast:

Andre d'Arnell . . . . Kenneth Kent

Lucille . . . . .Linden Travers

Danny . . . . Charles Maunsell

Freddy . . . . Preston Lockwood

Daisy . . . . Freda Falconer

ANDRE: Good evening, ladies and gentlemen. Permit me to introduce myself – Andre d'Arnell. (*Both surprised and amused*) What do I look like, madame? I am five feet ten. I have a small, but rather attractive moustache. My hair is dark and just a little – little touch of grey. And my clothes! Exciting!! Always exciting!! (*Politely*) Pardon? (*Puzzled*) Am I WHAT, monsieur? Marr-ied? Ah, oui! But of course! To an English girl. Her name is Lucille – she is twenty-nine and very, very chic. (*With a little laugh*) No, I do not know why she married me, madame, that is a mystery I have never been able to solve! However, tonight I have the honour to present to you the first of a series of weekly detective problems: Problems taken from my personal memoirs – the memoirs of Andre d'Arnell! So listen carefully, my friends, and see if you too can discover the mistake that the criminal made. (*After a moment*) One day, not so very long ago, Lucille and I were returning from a cocktail party. It was about eight o'clock in the evening (*START FADE*) and so dark that by the time we reached …

COMPLETE FADE.

CROSS FADE to the sound of a motor car. It is cruising at an average speed.

ANDRE: Well, did you enjoy the party, my sweet?

LUCILLE: It was terribly dull! (*Laughing*) And you talked far too much, Andre!

ANDRE: (*In high spirits*) Talked far too much! Of course I talked far too much, my pet. I always do. It's part of my personality.

LUCILLE: Yes – well, people don't expect it. (*Lightly*) Not from the celebrated Andre d'Arnell.

ANDRE: I know! They expect me to be strong and silent. (*Ponderously*) The – great – thoughtful – detective! (*Laughing*) Yes, well I don't like to be strong and silent. I like to be gay!!

LUCILLE: You were gay all right! Talk about a Sugar Daddy …

ANDRE: Lucille, please! You make me sound like an old man with a l-o-n-g white beard!

LUCILLE: (*Laughing*) Careful, darling – here's the drive!

The car slows down then gathers speed again.

ANDRE: (*Conversationally: after a pause*) That little girl was rather amusing I thought. The one with the pink …

LUCILLE: (*Suddenly: surprised*) Andre! Andre, there's something … stretching across the drive … Look … from that tree over there … Look!

ANDRE: (*Peering ahead*) I don't see anything … (*Laughing*) You've had too many cocktails I …(*Suddenly*) Mon dieu! Mon … (*Desperately*) Get your head down!! GET YOUR HEAD DOWN!!

There is a scream from LUCILLE.

The sudden screeching of brakes, the swerving of the car, and the smashing of glass.

After a moment the car rocks to a standstill.

ANDRE: (*After a pause: breathlessly*) Lucille! Lucille, are you all right?!

258

LUCILLE:	Y-Yes. Yes, Andre. I'm – I'm all right. (*Rather dazed*) But … But what happened?
ANDRE:	(*Seriously*) There's a wire-rope stretching right across the drive – it's fastened to that oak tree over on the left. (*Slowly*) If you hadn't noticed it, and I hadn't turned the car so that …
LUCILLE:	(*Quickly: tensely*) But the rope wasn't there at six o'clock. We came down the drive and …
ANDRE:	Exactly! (*Thoughtfully*) You know, Lucille, there are only two men in London who would think of a diabolical thing like that. Danny Roamer, and a man called Broderick – Freddy Broderick. Both have suffered in the past – as a result of my investigations – so I suppose they …
LUCILLE:	They … what …?
ANDRE:	I suppose they each have a pretty good reason for wishing to get rid of me.
LUCILLE:	You certainly have the nicest friends!
ANDRE:	(*Quietly: but with decision*) Go up to the house – change your dress – and bring the small car. I'll meet you at the gate.
LUCILLE:	But – But where are we going?
ANDRE:	Where do you think we're going, my sweet? To investigate of course. (*START FADE*) And don't keep me waiting because we have quite a little journey ahead of …

COMPLETE FADE.

CROSS FADE to ANDRE knocking on the door of a house.

LUCILLE:	You're not going to tell me that Danny Roamer actually lives in this dreadful little house! Why it isn't …

259

ANDRE: Ssh! (*Softly*) Taisez-vous …

The door is unbolted and opened.

DANNY: (*A bluff Irishman*) Who the dev …
           (*Surprised*) Why, hello, Frenchy! And what
           the devil brings the likes o' you round here
           this time o' night?

ANDRE: (*With quiet authority*) Hello, Danny! All
           alone?

DANNY: Sure! I've just come in from the local – from
           The Black Dog.

ANDRE: And where is this place – The Black Dog?

DANNY: T'is on the corner not two hundred yards
           away – and a more respectable little pub
           you'll not find this side o' Heaven.

ANDRE: And how long did you stay at this – this
           respectable little pub, Danny?

DANNY: From six o'clock until ten past nine. (*To
           LUCILLE*) T'is a lovely night I've had,
           mademoiselle! Drinkin' me favourite whisky
           an' dreamin' I was back in Ballybunion. And
           I ask ye now, is there a more genteel way of
           spending an evening?

ANDRE: Were you alone?

DANNY: No! No, bless ye – no! I've been with Freddy.
           You remember Freddy now – Freddy
           Broderick – a fine upstanding lad.

ANDRE: Yes. Yes, I remember Freddy. Come along,
           Lucille! I think we'll have a word with
           Monsieur Broderick. We'll – er – we'll see
           what that gentleman has got to say.

DANNY: And keep a civil tongue in your head,
           Frenchy, (*START FADE*) because there are
           times when poor old Freddy feels as if he's
           got to take the …

260

COMPLETE FADE.

*CROSS FADE to the background of a crowded and extremely
bawdy public house.*

FREDDY: (*A tough cockney*) Danny? Yus – 'ees been
            'ere all night – only left a few minutes ago.
            Ask Daisy, ask any o' the boys. If you think
            Danny's been up to something, Frenchy,
            you're barking up the wrong tree. Straight!
            I'm telling you straight!

ANDRE: And you, Freddy – how long have you been
            here?

FREDDY: Me? All night. That's right, isn't it, Daisy?

DAISY: (*A dreary cockney barmaid*) You seem to
            'ave been 'ere for weeks. What'll you 'ave?

ANDRE: A gin and Italian for my wife and ...

DAISY: No spirits – 'aven't 'ad any all night.
            (*Suddenly refined*) We can do you a very
            nice glass o' stout.

LUCILLE: I'm afraid I – I don't drink stout.

ANDRE: You'll drink it and like it, my sweet.
            (*Quickly, dismissing the barmaid*) O.K.
            O.K. Two stouts. (*Seriously*) Now listen,
            Freddy! Some misguided individual with a
            warped sense of humour attempted to
            murder me this evening. Now when it
            comes to murder, strange though it may
            seem my friend, I'm a pretty sensitive sort
            of guy – I – (*Almost with menace*) I don't
            like it!!

FREDDY: (*Extremely unpleasant*) What the 'ell are
            you getting at?

ANDRE: I'll tell you what I'm getting at, my friend! I
            know who put that rope across the drive. I

261

	know who attempted to murder Andre d'Arnell!!
FREDDY:	WHAT?!
LUCILLE:	(*Also astonished*) Andre! Andre. Are you joking?
ANDRE:	No my sweet – I'm not joking!

FADE UP music.
FADE DOWN.

| ANNOUNCER: | Who does Andre d'Arnell suspect? Do you know? Later in the programme we shall return you to Andre d'Arnell for the solution to tonight's detective problem. |

Turn over for the solution to mystery one.

MYSTERY ONE – THE SOLUTION

ANNOUNCER: We now return you to Andre d'Arnell for the solution to tonight's detective problem.

FREDDY: WHAT?!

LUCILLE: (*Also astonished*) Andre! Andre. Are you joking?

ANDRE: (*Slowly*) No my sweet – I'm not joking!

FREDDY: (*Shaken*) Well, if you're not joking, Mr Clever – What's the game?

ANDRE: (*Slowly: with almost menace*) I am going to give you and Danny twenty-four hours! Twenty-four hours to make yourself scarce! If you don't there'll be a warrant out – a warrant for the arrest of …

FREDDY: (*Suddenly: desperately*) I had nothing to do with it! I swear I had nothin' to do with it! It was Danny – he made me promise to provide him with an alibi and then …

ANDRE: Yes. Yes, I know it was Danny …

FREDDY: (*Bewildered*) But – But how do you know?

LUCILLE: Yes, Andre, how do you know it was – Danny?

ANDRE: Didn't you hear what Danny said, my sweet? He said that he'd spent the evening here – at The Black Dog – drinking … drinking his … his favourite whisky.

LUCILLE: Well?

ANDRE: But you heard Daisy, the barmaid! How could Danny drink his favourite whisky? There hasn't been any whisky all night. No spirits – no spirits at all!

FREDDY:	Well, I'm … Coo, an' we thought we 'ad the perfect alibi!
ANDRE:	(*Pleased with himself: animated*) There is no such thing as the perfect alibi, my friend. In the art of criminal deduction it is always necessary to take into consideration the fundamental principles governing the psychological reaction of …
LUCILLE:	Andre!
ANDRE:	Yes, my sweet?
LUCILLE:	You're talking too much!
ANDRE:	(*Delighted with himself*) But of course!!!

FADE UP of closing music.

MYSTERY TWO

Cast:

Andre d'Arnell . . . . Kenneth Kent
Lucille . . . . .Linden Travers
Hotel Manager . . . . .Fred Yule
Rogers . . . . Dermot Cathie

As the opening music finishes CROSS FADE to ANDRE d'ARNELL.

ANDRE: Good evening, ladies and gentlemen. Tonight I have the honour to present to you another detective problem. A problem taken from my personal memoirs – the memoirs of Andre d'Arnell. So listen carefully my friends and see if you too can discover the mistake that the criminal made. (*After a moment*) Many months ago, Lucille and I were staying in London. We were staying (*START FADE*) at a small hotel not so very far away from Park Lane. I remember the occasion well because by a strange ...

FADE SCENE.

CROSS FADE TO LUCILLE.

LUCILLE: Andre!

ANDRE: Yes, my darling?

LUCILLE: You look awful. You can't possibly wear a pink shirt with a blue suit. It isn't done.

ANDRE: (*In high spirits*) Listen, Lucille, today is my birthday. I am thirty-nine. So if I want to wear a pink shirt with a blue suit then ...

LUCILLE: Forty-three.

ANDRE: Pardon?

LUCILLE: Forty-three, Andre.

ANDRE: (*Quietly*) Well, I – er – I feel like thirty-nine.

A telephone rings. ANDRE lifts the receiver.

ANDRE: Hello? ... Yes, speaking ... (*Impatiently*) Pardon? ... (*With dignity*) Monsieur, there is only one Andre d'Arnell! ... Yes, yes, of course I am listening. (*Pause – seriously*) When did this happen? (*Softly*) Oh. Oh, I see. (*Briskly*) Yes – yes, of course. At once, Monsieur Le Directeur!

The receiver is replaced.

LUCILLE: (*Quietly – tensely*) What is it, Andre?

ANDRE: (*Thoughtfully – slowly*) Lucille, do you remember, yesterday afternoon … there was a girl in the lounge – a rather pretty girl – she wore a green dress, a diamond necklace, and …

LUCILLE: And she smiled at you, my sweet – rather unnecessarily I thought.

ANDRE: Did she, my pet. It must have been my new suit! (*After a moment – with a sigh*) Ah, well … I'm afraid she won't … smile … again, poor darling.

LUCILLE: What do you mean?

ANDRE: She was discovered in her room this morning by the chambermaid … dead … strangled to death. The necklace is missing …

LUCILLE: Oh. Oh, how horrible!

ANDRE: Come along, my sweet – I'm going to have a chat with the manager. (*Impatiently*) Come along. Come along! (*START FADE*) Depechez-vous … Depechez vous …

FADE SCENE.

CROSS FADE to the MANAGER: Just at the moment it is rather difficult to hear what he is saying because of a background of dance music.

MANAGER: I knew that you were staying in the hotel, Monsieur d'Arnell, so I naturally thought – well – under the circumstances surely …

ANDRE: (*Unable to hear*) Pardon, monsieur?

MANAGER: (*Raising his voice: he is also very nervous*) I – I said, I knew that you were staying in the hotel, Monsieur d'Arnell, so I …

ROGERS: I'll close the top window, sir – oddly enough you can't hear the music then.

The window is closed and the music can no longer be heard.

MANAGER: (*With almost a sigh of relief*) Ah. Ah, that's better!

ANDRE: Now, Monsieur Le Directeur, if you please – the details ...

MANAGER: Well, er – this young lady, Miss – Miss Philips, arrived here yesterday morning. She booked this room about a fortnight ago.

ANDRE: Had she stayed with you before?

MANAGER: No. No, never.

ANDRE: And this gentleman, who closed the window?

MANAGER: Oh, er – this is Mr Rogers. He took Miss Philips to the theatre last night. When I heard what had happened I – I thought it best for me to get in touch with him.

ANDRE: You knew ... Mademoiselle Philips, monsieur?

ROGERS: Yes – but not very well I'm afraid. You see, Miss Philips was a friend of my sister's. She came up to Town for a few days and my sister wrote and asked me if I'd look after her. We met last night for the first time.

ANDRE: Where did you meet?

ROGERS: In the cocktail bar.

ANDRE: At what time, monsieur?

ROGERS: Oh – I should say at about a quarter past six. After one or two drinks we went straight to the theatre.

ANDRE: And what time was it when you returned – to the hotel?

271

ROGERS:	As a matter of fact I didn't come back to the hotel. I put Miss Philips into a taxi at Oxford Circus.
ANDRE:	I see. Now, Monsieur Le Directeur, tell me, how did you know that Monsieur Rogers was a friend of Mademoiselle Philips? Do you frequent this particular hotel, Monsieur Rogers?
ROGERS:	No, no. Last night was the first time I'd ever been in the hotel. But Mr Bradman here, the Manager, introduced ...
MANAGER:	I introduced myself – last night – in the cocktail bar. When I heard about the murder I remembered Mr Rogers' name and I looked it up in the telephone book.
ANDRE:	Oh, oh, I see.
MANAGER:	It was the chambermaid that discovered the murder, Monsieur d'Arnell, so if you'd like to ...
ANDRE:	My wife is talking to the chambermaid; but there is one more question I would like to ask you, Monsieur Le Directeur. (*Start SLOW FADE*) Now, tell me, when you first heard that Mademoiselle Philips had been murdered what was your immediate reaction? Did you decide to communicate with ...

FADE SCENE.

CROSS FADE to a door opening and closing.

ANDRE:	Hello, Lucille. Did you see the chambermaid?
LUCILLE:	(*Imitating the maid*) Yes, an' she's proper North Country. (*Laughing*) In future you can do your own dirty work, Andre.
ANDRE:	What did she say?

LUCILLE:	Well, apparently, this maid went into the bedroom at about half past ten this morning, drew back the curtains, opened the window, and then …
ANDRE:	… discovered the body? M'm.
LUCILLE:	Andre, when do you think the murder was committed?
ANDRE:	I should say just before midnight. There was a wristlet watch on mademoiselle's wrist. It had obviously stopped during the course of the struggle. It said ten minutes to twelve.
LUCILLE:	Why are you smiling?
ANDRE:	I was just thinking, Lucille. Always, in a case of this kind, you come up against the perfect alibi. Monsieur Bradman, the manager, states that from ten o'clock until midnight he was in the ballroom listening to the dance orchestra. There's been a little trouble with the orchestra, that's why they were practising this morning. The other person, a young man by the name of Rogers, states that he left mademoiselle at roughly about a quarter past nine. By ten fifteen – he was in bed.
LUCILLE:	(*Puzzled*) Well – er – what do you think, Andre?
ANDRE:	(*Slowly – amused*) I think … I think that one of them is not … exactly … telling … the truth. (*He chuckles*)
LUCILLE:	(*Astonished*) You – you know who murdered … Miss Philips!
ANDRE:	Of course I know, my pet. Someone told me.
LUCILLE:	(*Amazed*) Someone – told – you! Who?
ANDRE:	You did, my sweetie pie! (*He chuckles again*)

FADE UP of music.

273

FADE DOWN.

ANNOUNCER: Who does Andre d'Arnell suspect? Do you know? Later in the programme you will hear from Andre d'Arnell himself the solution to tonight's detective problem.

Turn over for the solution to mystery two.

ANNOUNCER: We now return you to Andre d'Arnell for the solution to tonight's detective problem.

LUCILLE: (*Amazed*) Someone – told – you! Who?

ANDRE: You did, my sweetie pie! (*He chuckles again*)

LUCILLE: I – I did!

ANDRE: Yes. You made me think of something. Something I'd almost forgotten. You see, you told me that when the maid went into the bedroom this morning she opened the window.

LUCILLE: Yes?

ANDRE: Well, that made me think of a certain … a certain … chance … remark. A certain chance remark made by Monsieur Rogers!

LUCILLE: Well?

ANDRE: The young man claims that he met Mademoiselle Philips in the cocktail bar and then went straight back to the theatre. He states that he did <u>not</u> come back to the hotel.

LUCILLE: Well. What are you getting at?

ANDRE: I'm getting at the fact that he did come back to the hotel and that, for a time at any rate, he was in the bedroom!

LUCILLE: How do you know this?

ANDRE: (*Slowly*) I know it, my dear Lucille, because when he closed the window he said, "I'll close the top window, sir – oddly enough you can't hear the music then." Don't you get the significance of that remark? He'd closed that window <u>once before</u>!

276

LUCILLE:	Andre. Andre! You're a genius!
ANDRE:	(*Pleased with himself*) Thank you, my pet!
LUCILLE:	(*Horrified*) But that dreadful shirt! (*With an exasperated sigh*) Oh, oh, if only you hadn't such appalling taste!
ANDRE:	(*Chirpily*) I married you, my sweet! (*He chuckles*)

FADE UP of closing music.

MYSTERY THREE

Cast:

Andre d'Arnell . . . . Kenneth Kent

Lucille . . . . Linden Travers

Fred . . . . Dick Francis

Kerr . . . . Fred Yule

As the opening music finishes CROSS FADE to d'ARNELL.

ANDRE: Good evening, ladies and gentlemen. Tonight I have the honour to present to you another detective problem. A problem taken from my personal memoirs – the memoirs of Andre d'Arnell. So listen carefully, my friends, and see if you, too, can discover the mistake that the criminal made. (*After a moment*) Two or three months ago, when Lucille and I were staying in London, we had an experience which was – well – to say the least – extraordinary. We had rented an apartment in a block of service flats just off Pall Mall, and one night – it would be about a quarter past eleven – I was explaining to Lucille how (*START FADE*) I had the good fortune to solve one of …

FADE SCENE.

FADE IN of d'ARNELL talking.

ANDRE: So you see, my darling, it was only by close observation, systematic research, and a determination on my part not to be hoodwinked by the conventional aspects of the case that ultimately determined … (*Suddenly*) Lucille, are you asleep?

LUCILLE: (*Yawning*) No … no, Andre, I'm listening.

ANDRE: Well, as I was saying, it was only by close observation, systematic research, and a determination on my part not to … Lucille! Lucille, you're not listening!

LUCILLE: (*Weary*) Andre, we've been in bed for hours – won't you ever stop talking?

ANDRE: (*Surprised*) Don't you like me to talk in bed?

281

LUCILLE:	Not all the time, darling – please!
ANDRE:	Lucille, you are so strong! Oh, so strange. I tell you one of the most exciting …
LUCILLE:	(*Suddenly – wide awake*) Andre. Andre! Listen!
ANDRE:	What is it?
LUCILLE:	(*Tensely*) Listen!

In the street below voices are heard: excited voices: people shouting: fire engines are heard: a bell is clanging.

ANDRE:	(*Suddenly, staggered*) Lucille! Lucille!
LUCILLE:	(*Frightened*) What is it, Andre, what's happened?
ANDRE:	(*Quickly – excited*) Don't you smell it?!! It's fire! The building's on fire!
LUCILLE:	On – on fire!
ANDRE:	Wait here, my darling! No … no, don't follow me! Get your dressing gown – wait here!
LUCILLE:	(*Terrified*) Andre, don't leave me! Don't – don't leave me, Andre! (*Desperately*) Andre!

FADE UP of street noises; the noise of the fire and falling masonry.

ANDRE:	(*Breathlessly*) Lucille – we're in a pretty warm spot – six floors up and no means of getting down! The staircase has gone – the emergency staircase is right over on the other side!
LUCILLE:	Can – can we get there?
ANDRE:	I – I doubt it, my sweet!
LUCILLE:	What – what are we going to do?
ANDRE:	I don't know. It seems to me that our only …
LUCILLE:	(*Terrified*) Andre, what are we going to do?
ANDRE:	Now, Lucille, for goodness sake don't let yourself get …
FRED:	(*From the near background – a typical Cockney*) Look out! Keep clear o' the window!

There's a sudden smashing of glass. Fire crackles through the following dialogue.

ANDRE: (*With relief*) Are we glad to see you, my friend!

FRED: Blimey, it's getting a bit warm, isn't it?

LUCILLE: Andre! Andre – I'll never be able to climb down that ladder! Look at the height! Look at …

ANDRE: Now don't be silly, Lucille … don't be silly … It's not so very high … it's only … (*Nervously*) … only six storeys!

FRED: (*Briskly*) Come on, miss! Come on! Pull that bit o' chiffon round you – let's get cracking.

LUCILLE: I – I can't do it! I can-t – can-t … (*Weakly*) Oh! (*She faints*)

ANDRE: (*Alarmed*) She's fainted! Lucille! Lucille!

FRED: 'Ere, I'll get hold of 'er, and … (*Tensely*) It's all right, mate. I'll get 'old of 'er – you jump to it! Come on, miss – on my shoulder.

ANDRE: Oh, no you don't, my friend! Not with all those people watching! If anyone makes the grand exit, it's going to be Andre d'Arnell! Come along – on my shoulder, darling! Steady! Steady!

LUCILLE: (*Weakly*) Take it – take it slowly, Andre!

ANDRE: (*Staggering*) You can depend on that, my sweet!

FADE UP of street noises.

FADE SCENE completely.

FADE Up of ANDRE.

ANDRE: Another whisky and soda, Inspector?

KERR: No, I – I don't think so – thank you very much, sir. (*Pleasantly*) Sorry about your foot, Mrs

	d'Arnell – here, let me get you that cushion – is it very painful?
LUCILLE:	No – not when I'm resting. (*With a little laugh*) This would never have happened you know if Andre hadn't tried to show off.
ANDRE:	Darling.
LUCILLE:	(*Sweetly – to annoy ANDRE*) He jumped, Inspector, off the last rung – just to impress the crowd.
ANDRE:	Darling, I swear. I swear to you I slipped! Inspector, I was putting my best foot forward when suddenly I – I – I went tipsy-topsy, I mean topsy-tipsy, I mean turvy-tea …. I slipped!

The INSPECTOR and LUCILLE laugh.

KERR:	Anyway, you were certainly both very lucky. Now, Monsieur d'Arnell … (*He clears his throat*) We have reason to suspect – pretty good reason too – that that fire was started deliberately, that it was, in fact, a case of arson.
LUCILLE:	Arson?
KERR:	Exactly!
ANDRE:	(*Quietly*) Go on, Inspector.
KERR:	As you probably know, the building belongs to a moneylender by the name of Sanray – Gabriel Sanray. Now, Sanray isn't exactly a popular sort of person so …
LUCILLE:	He certainly isn't, Inspector!
KERR:	… so we've had a little difficulty narrowing down the field of suspects. However, we now feel pretty convinced that the fire was started either by our old friend Teddy Ryan or by another gentleman by the name of Oakes – Spider Oakes.

ANDRE: What time was the fire actually started – do you know?

KERR: Yes – shortly before a quarter past eleven. I had a chat with Ryan this morning and he tells me that at a quarter past eleven last night he was in the tube travelling from Piccadilly Circus to Marble Arch.

ANDRE: Where did he spend the earlier part of the evening?

KERR: I'll give you the exact details. Now let me see – he left his flat at about six forty-five and went straight to a public house called The Happy Mermaid – that's on the Tottenham Court Road. He left the pub at about nine o'clock and took a taxi down to a club in Piccadilly. He claims to have left Piccadilly just before eleven. He fell asleep as soon as the train started – he was pretty tight – and only just managed to wake up when the train reached his destination.

ANDRE: And what about the other gentleman – Spider Oakes?

KERR: Apparently, Spider's friendly with a girl who works in the pay-box at a suburban cinema – The Royalty Cinema in Wimbledon. He went out there last night at about seven o'clock and arrived back in the west end just after midnight.

ANDRE: Did he see the programme?

KERR: Oh, yes. He saw the programme all right. He said it was an old film of James Cagney's ... t't ... now what was it called? Oh, I remember – Enemies of the Public.

ANDRE: Enemies of the Public. An appropriate picture for our friend.

285

LUCILLE: But Spider couldn't have spent the entire evening from seven o'clock until ... (*Suddenly – puzzled*) Why are you smiling, Andre?

ANDRE: (*Pleased with himself*) How many times have I told you, my darling, that it is the small, trivial, and apparently unimportant little points which invariably indicate the true state of ...

LUCILLE: (*Staggered*) Andre! Andre – you – you – know ...?

ANDRE: But, of course!

FADE UP of music.
FADE DOWN.

ANNOUNCER: Who does Andre d'Arnell think started the fire? Later in the programme we will return you to Andre d'Arnell himself for the solution to tonight's detective problem.

Turn over the page for the solution to mystery three.

MYSTERY THREE – THE SOLUTION

ANNOUNCER: We now return you to Andre d'Arnell for the solution to tonight's detective problem.

LUCILLE: (*Staggered*) Andre! Andre – you – you – know …?

ANDRE: But, of course!

KERR: But – but, God bless my soul, how do you know?

ANDRE: My friend, observe with intelligence please the statement made by our old friend Teddy Ryan. He claims to have entered the train at Piccadilly Circus, to have fallen asleep, and to have awakened – just in the nick of time – at his destination: Marble Arch. But, my dear Inspector, if you take a train from Piccadilly Circus to Marble Arch you've got to change. How could Mr Ryan do this if he was fast asleep?

KERR: (*Annoyed with himself*) Well, I'll be …

ANDRE: No! No! No, my friend. Just make up your mind that in future you will devote to the small and apparently trivial details the same meticulous thought and careful consideration that you invariably …

LUCILLE: Andre!

ANDRE: I know, my darling! I know. I'm talking too much! I always do!

FADE UP of music.

MYSTERY FOUR
Cast:

Andre d'Arnell . . . . Kenneth Kent
Lucille . . . . .Linden Travers
A Waiter . . . . Dermot Cathie
Lady Waverley . . . . .Josephine Shand

As the opening music finishes CROSS FADE to d'ARNELL.

ANDRE: Good evening, my friends. Tonight Lucille has asked me to tell the strange story of Lady Waverley; so listen carefully and see if you too, like Andre d'Arnell, can discover the mistake that was made by ... (*Significantly*) ... that was made by a certain person. (*After a moment*) One night, many months ago, Lucille and I were dining at the Ritz. We had finished dinner and had started to dance – (*With conceit: aside*) I dance so beautifully you know, and with such a perfect sense of rhythm! – when suddenly one of the waiters happened to (*START FADE*) catch my eye. At first I did not realise that he wanted to speak with me but gradually ...

COMPLETE FADE.

FADE UP the noise of people dancing and this continues throughout the following dialogue.

LUCILLE: Andre!

ANDRE: (*Dancing with LUCILLE, pleased with himself*) Yes, my darling?

LUCILLE: Don't jig so much!

ANDRE: (*Horrified*) Jig! JIG, you say!!! My sweet, I dance like an angel! Why my pirouettes are absolutely exquisite!

LUCILLE: You dance like a baby elephant with a violent attack of hiccups, and for goodness sake Andre don't ...

ANDRE: (*Interrupting LUCILLE after the word 'hiccup'*) I know you're jealous, my darling, I know you're jealous!! Why I've seen the day when ... (*Complete change of voice*) What the

devil is that fellow nodding his head about –
that waiter over there …

As ANDRE speaks the dance orchestra stops: there is a smattering of applause.

LUCILLE: He's coming over here.

WAITER: Pardon, monsieur. Monsieur d'Arnell?

ANDRE: Yes.

WAITER: Lady Waverley presents her compliments, monsieur, and would esteem it an honour if madam and yourself would join her for – for a moment or two.

LUCILLE: (*Puzzled*) Lady Waverley?

WAITER: (*Lowering his voice*) The old lady with the white hair, madam – in the corner – near the alcove.

LUCILLE: Oh … Oh, yes …

ANDRE: (*Quietly*) Come along, Lucille. (*Aside: to the WAITER*) Thank you, waiter. (*To LUCILLE*) Come along, my darling, we'll see what (*START FADE*) this distinguished old lady has got to say for herself …

FADE SCENE.

CROSS FADE TO LADY WAVERLEY.

LADY W: (*Very old, but quite a gentle and kind voice*) Now do have another glass of wine, my dear. Please! Please! I insist!

LUCILLE: (*With a little laugh*) No, I won't just now – if you don't mind.

ANDRE: (*Interrupting LUCILLE*) Lady Waverley, forgive me if I sound a little impatient, but you have not yet told me why – (*He speaks slowly: obviously studying LADY WAVERLEY very*

	closely) Why you wanted to talk with Andre d'Arnell?
LADY W:	(*Pleasantly*) You have a reputation you know, Monsieur d'Arnell – a reputation for being probably the most famous detective in Europe.
ANDRE:	(*Shocked*) PROBABLY, madame! Tut! Tut! Tut! Tut!
LUCILLE:	(*Amused*) The most conceited – certainly!
LADY W:	(*Lightly: laughing*) Monsieur has a right to be conceited.
ANDRE:	I think so too, dear lady, but … but you still have not answered my question?
LADY W:	(*After a moment: tensely*) I'm in trouble … great trouble … there are times in fact when I feel so desperate that I could almost … (*Pulling herself together*) However, I – I suppose I'd better start my story at the beginning.
ANDRE:	It is always an advantage, madame …
LADY W:	Twelve years ago, in the autumn of 1932, my oldest boy – Ronnie – committed suicide. After his death we discovered that he had been receiving, over a period of many months, a series of anonymous, blackmailing, – I suppose you'd call them poison-pen – letters. At the time I consulted my brother – I'm a widow you know – and we decided, rather foolishly perhaps, not to … (*She hesitates*)
ANDRE:	Not to consult Scotland Yard.
LADY W:	(*Softly*) Yes.
ANDRE:	Go on, madame …
LADY W:	(*Slowly*) Two days ago, Monsieur d'Arnell, I too received a letter – it had been placed, rather mysteriously, on my dressing table. (*With an effort*) It was exactly the same sort of letter that

293

	– that Ronnie received … and the writer demanded … nine hundred pounds.
LUCILLE:	(*Puzzled*) But supposing you refuse to pay this nine hundred pounds what exactly does this – this person threaten you <u>with</u>? I mean, surely …
LADY W:	We are an old and distinguished family, my dear. And like many old and distinguished families there have been incidents in the past which … which we should prefer not to have published.
ANDRE:	Madame, tell me, do you think this letter – the one you received two days ago – was written by the same person that wrote the anonymous letters to your son?
LADY W:	I'm sure of it, Monsier d'Arnell. You see, I've had the handwriting examined – examined by an expert.
ANDRE:	Oh! Oh – and what did this expert tell you?
LADY W:	He told me that in his opinion the letters were identical – that although the handwriting had been disguised – the letters were quite obviously written by the same person.
ANDRE:	Lady Waverley, tell me: what does your household consist of: who is living with you at the moment?
LADY W:	Well – there's my sister-in-law Charlotte – that's Mrs Marsham, there's Beatrice the housekeeper, and my maid – a Canadian girl by the name of Carson – Janet Carson.
LUCILLE:	How long has Miss Carson been with you?
LADY W:	About five years; but I'm afraid neither Janet, nor my sister-in-law for that matter, could possibly have written the letters to my son.

ANDRE:	Oh? Oh – and why not?
LADY W:	Well, you see, they were both out of the country during 1932, and the letters to Ronnie were quite obviously delivered by hand. Actually Janet only came over here for the first time in '36.
LUCILLE:	Had she good references?
LADY W:	Oh, excellent, my dear. She worked her passage from America – as a stewardess on The Queen Mary – and then I believe stayed with a Scots family in Glasgow for a short while. She came to me in August, 1940.
ANDRE:	And your sister-in-law? Where was Mrs Marsham during 1932?
LADY W:	In Switzerland. As a matter of fact she lived there until her husband died – just before the outbreak of this war. They had rather a lovely place I believe, although I never saw it. It was in the mountains, according to Charlotte, near … near … Now, what did they call the place? Dear – Dear, my memory! Oh! Oh, I remember – near Murron.
ANDRE:	Oh, yes! (*Deep in thought*) Yes, I know … I know that district quite well …
LUCILLE:	(*After a moment: quietly*) Andre!
ANDRE:	(*Suddenly: pulling himself together*) Yes, my darling?
LUCILLE:	(*Amused*) You look rather perplexed!
ANDRE:	(*Very brightly*) I'm not perplexed, my sweet! I feel quite chirpy!
LADY W:	(*Obviously very worried*) Monsieur d'Arnell I – I – don't wish to put you to any trouble, or any inconvenience at all, but – but if you

295

	think you could possibly discover who wrote those letters then I – I – I should be eternally grateful.
ANDRE:	But my dear Lady Waverley, I know who wrote those letters! (*Amused*) Oh, it is so simple!
LUCILLE:	Andre, you – you – know?
LADY W:	(*Staggered*) You – You – You know?
ANDRE:	But of course!

FADE up of music.
FADE DOWN.

| ANNOUNCER: | Who does Andre d'Arnell suspect? Do you know? Later in the programme we shall return you to Andre d'Arnell for the solution to tonight's detective problem. |

Turn over the page to read the solution to mystery four.

MYSTERY FOUR – THE SOLUTION

ANNOUNCER: We now return you to Andre d'Arnell for the solution to tonight's detective problem.

LUCILLE: Andre, you – you – know?

LADY W: (*Staggered*) You – You – You know?

ANDRE: But of course!

LADY W: (*Bewildered*) But I don't see how you could possibly know, why ...

ANDRE: (*Pleased with himself*) My dear Lady Waverley, in a case of this sort it is only necessary for a person of my intelligence to take into careful consideration the apparently unimportant and trivial details governing the circumstances leading up to the ...

LUCILLE: Andre!

ANDRE: (*Recognising the tone of LUCILLE's voice*) Yes, my sweet?

LUCILLE: If you are going to honour us with an explanation would you mind ... (*Sweetly*) ... In basic English?

ANDRE: My darling, it's not a question of basic English – it's a question of basic common sense. The maid – what do you call her? – Janet Carson?: she is obviously telling a pack of lies from start to finish. I ask you, my darling – how could she come over on The Queen Mary in 1936 – the maiden voyage was not until May, 1937!

LADY W: (*Stunned*) Why – why – (*Terribly grateful*) Monsieur d'Arnell, I – I – I think you're a genius!

298

ANDRE: (*Completely casually*) Thank you, madame. I think so too!

LUCILLE: (*In a good humour, but this time overwhelmed by ANDRE's conceit*) Why you conceited, self-satisfied, bombastic ...

ANDRE: (*Playfully shocked*) Darling! Darling! Please!!

FADE UP of music.

MYSTERY FIVE
Cast:

Andre d'Arnell . . . . Kenneth Kent
Lucille . . . . .Linden Travers
Thornton Reece . . . . Lewis Stringer
Dr Canterbury . . . . .Foster Carlin
Inspector Dawson . . . . .Arthur Ridley
Major Thorne . . . . Fred Yule

As the opening music finishes CROSS FADE to d'ARNELL.

ANDRE: Good evening, my friends. Now listen very carefully to my problem tonight and see if you too, like Andre d'Arnell, can discover the mistake that the criminal made. (*After a moment*) Shortly after I made my little slip about the Queen Mary – it was 1936 you know – Lucille and I visited an art exhibition in New Bond Street. It was held by a gentleman by the name of Thornton Reece. I had read quite a lot about the work of this new artist and when we arrived at the gallery an artistic young gentleman introduced himself. We also noticed a quiet, insignificant little man by the name of Canterbury – er – Dr George Canterbury.

COMPLETE FADE.

LUCILLE: Andre, isn't this a <u>lovely</u> picture of the Queen Mary. And painted in 1936 too.

ANDRE: My darling, I beseech you, don't mention that boat to me! I'm desolate.

LUCILLE: (*Laughing*) But you can't always by right, Andre.

ANDRE: Move along, my darling – don't let's look at the picture – move along!

LUCILLE: Oh, this is nice! Andre, we shall simply have to buy this!

ANDRE: It's a hundred guineas, my sweet.

LUCILLE: (*Thrilled*) Yes, I know, but – but it's so original!

ANDRE: I'm – I'm glad you think so, Lucille.

LUCILLE: But – but don't you?

ANDRE:	Oh, it's original, my pet! Most original! But – er – but what is it exactly?
LUCILLE:	Don't be silly, Andre. You can see what it is – it's perfectly obvious.
ANDRE:	Well – what is it?
LUCILLE:	Why, it's – er – sort of – er – kind of – er – you know – a sort of … Andre, it's obvious.
ANDRE:	It ought to be a great deal more obvious than that, my darling, for one hundred guineas!
CANTERBURY:	(*Pleasantly – rather humble in manner*) Forgive me, sir, I – er – I couldn't help but overhear your remark. The catalogue describes No 16 as The Waltz of Destiny.
LUCILLE:	(*Astonished*) The Waltz of Destiny!
ANDRE:	(*Amused*) You seem strangely surprised, my dear.
LUCILLE:	Yes, I – I must confess I didn't exactly think it was … The Waltz of Destiny …
REECE:	(*A slightly Welsh accent*) Number 16 is sold, but may I draw your attention to Number 24, sir?
ANDRE:	Ah, yes! Yes, now that's most interesting …
CANTERBURY:	Green Hedges … M'm … M'm … rather an odd sort of title for a picture of …

CANTERBURY is interrupted by the opening and closing of a door and the entrance of MAJOR THORNE.

THORNE:	(*Extremely hot headed – bad tempered*) Is this the so-called Thornton Reece exhibition?
REECE:	Yes, sir.

THORNE:	I don't suppose you happen to be this fellow Thornton Reece by any chance? No, of course you wouldn't be. Too respectable looking.
REECE:	Yes, my name is Thornton Reece. What can I do for you now?
THORNE:	I've brought this thing back, sir! My son bought it yesterday morning. Silly ass must have been tight! Tight as a badger!
REECE:	You don't like the picture?
THORNE:	I certainly don't like it, an' what's more I don't like the thought of my son paying fifty quid for it! Here we are – take the rotten thing – and let me have a cheque by tomorrow morning! Major Thorne, Cranstairs Club, Pall Mall.

The door opens.

THORNE:	(*Briskly*) Out of my way, sir!
DAWSON:	(*Rather heavy in manner – officious*) One moment, sir, if you don't mind.
THORNE:	(*Indignantly*) Leave go of my arm! Who – who the devil do you think you are, sir?
DAWSON:	Inspector Dawson, C.I.D. (*Aside*) Close the door, sergeant.

The door closes.

DAWSON:	Now if you don't mind standing on one (*Suddenly*) Why, hello Mr d'Arnell – I didn't expect to find you here!
ANDRE:	You appear to be quite perturbed, Inspector. What seems to be the trouble?
DAWSON:	(*Briskly*) A valuable diamond pendant has been stolen, sir. Jewellers corner o' Brook Street.
ANDRE:	Oh? (*Interested*) Oh, when did this happen?
DAWSON:	About fifteen minutes ago, sir. The man got away – we're under the impression he's still in the district.

LUCILLE:	Did you see him, Inspector?
DAWSON:	No, I'm afraid we didn't, ma'am. (*Rather brisk*) You're Thornton Reece, I take it. How long have these people been in here, Mr Reece? I don't mean this lady and gentlemen – Mr and Mrs d'Arnell.
REECE:	Well, now, let me think … The place was empty for about fifteen minutes and then … and then this gentleman dropped in. That would be roughly about – about, I should say, ten minutes ago. Shortly afterwards Mr and Mrs – d'Arnell did you say – arrived.
CANTERBURY:	Yes, yes, that's quite correct. My name is Dr Canterbury, Inspector. Dr George Canterbury.
DAWSIN:	And this gentleman?
LUCILLE:	This gentleman has only just arrived. His name is Major Thorne, Inspector.
ANDRE:	Yes. (*Pleasantly*) By the way, is that your taxi outside, Major?
THORNE:	Yes – and you can have a word with the driver if you like. Picked him up in Hammersmith about twenty minutes ago. Came straight here.
DAWSON:	What did you come here for – just to see the exhibition?
THORNE:	I did not, sir! I've brought this picture back – me son bought it yesterday morning – paid fifty quid for it! Fifty quid, mark you!
DAWSON:	(*Puzzled*) What – what is it exactly?

THORNE:	By gad, sir – you might well ask! D'you hear that, Reece? What is it? And he's a detective!
REECE:	(*Annoyed*) I should have thought it was perfectly obvious what it was! It's a copy of the famous painting The Scapegoat by Rossetti.
THORNE:	The Scapegoat! Yes – well you're not making a scapegoat out of me, sir! Or my son if it comes to that!
LUCILLE:	Well, I think it's an awfully good copy, Mr Reece.
REECE:	(*Offended by THORNE*) Thank you, madam.
THORNE:	(*Quite brightly*) Yes – well – there you are, Inspector. I came straight here from Hammersmith. The taxi never stopped – not once. (*A bluff manner*) So I couldn't very well have pinched your precious pendant, could I?
DAWSON:	No, sir.
ANDRE:	(*Almost amused*) And what about you, doctor? Did you come straight here from – from Hammersmith?
CANTERBURY:	I'm – I'm afraid I didn't, sir. I got out of the tube in Oxford Street about twenty minutes ago – and simply strolled down New Bond Street. I'm – I'm afraid you've only got my word for it … of course.
ANDRE:	(*Quite pleasantly*) No one wishes to doubt your word, monsieur, but that isn't a particularly good alibi, now is it?
CANTERBURY:	No. No, I suppose it isn't.

DAWSON: (*About to leave*) Yes, well – if you'll give the sergeant full details, doctor, with regard to your personal …

ANDRE: One moment, Inspector. Please. If you don't mind.

DAWSON: (*Surprised*) What is it, sir?

ANDRE: I hope you will not think it presumption, monsieur, but I should like, with your permission of course, to offer just a little – little word of advice. In a case of this sort, Monsieur Le Commissioner, it is not only necessary to keep the ears – what do you say? – awake? Always listen to the little things, monsieur. (*Carried away*) It is the little things – the chance remark, the nod, the wink – which have invariably an important bearing upon the ultimate outcome of any …

LUCILLE: (*Interrupting ANDRE*) Andre!

ANDRE: (*Recognising LUCILLE's tone*) Yes, my sweet?

LUCILLE: You're talking too much!

ANDRE: Of course I'm talking too much, my darling. You know why. I'm excited … and ask me why I'm excited, my pet. I'll tell you. I'm excited because (*With sudden seriousness*) … because I know who stole the diamond pendant.

DAWSON: What!!!

LUCILLE: Andre!!!

THORNE: By Gad, sir, are you going to calmly stand there (*START FADE*) and tell us that you actually know who stole the diamond pendant!!!

FADE UP of music.
FADE DOWN.

ANNOUNCER: Do you know who stole the diamond pendant? Later in the programme we shall return you to Andre d'Arnell for the solution to tonight's detective problem.

Sadly the solution to mystery five no longer exists but can you solve the mystery as you think Andre d'Arnell did?

MYSTERY SIX
Cast:

Andre d'Arnell . . . . Kenneth Kent

Lucille . . . . Linden Travers

Wilson . . . . Dermot Cathie

Charlie . . . . Fred Yule

As the opening music finishes CROSS FADE to ANDRE d'ARNELL.

ANDRE: Tonight, my friends, I propose to tell you of what happened in the city of Liverpool on a certain Saturday afternoon in October last year. Now listen carefully to this problem and see if you too, like Andre d'Arnell, can discover the mistake that the criminal made. (*After a moment*) Lucille and I, on this particular Saturday afternoon, were walking down an extremely pleasant little street not so very far away from the Art Gallery. Suddenly Lucille noticed – in the window of a small jewellers – a particularly charming diamond bracelet. (*START FADE*) I thought myself the bracelet was rather charming but when I noticed the price I must confess my heart went ...

FADE.

FADE UP LUCILLE.

LUCILLE: Andre, isn't it lovely!

ANDRE: Yes, darling – but two hundred guineas! Now, I ask you!

LUCILLE: Well, after all, Andre, you haven't bought me anything – not recently.

ANDRE: What about the fur coat, my sweet? What about the sapphire ring? What about the new hat?

LUCILLE: Which new hat?

ANDRE: The one you're wearing!

LUCILLE: Well – you said you didn't like it!

ANDRE: I don't like it, my sweetie-pie – but I've got to pay for it!

LUCILLE: (*Laughing*) Yes, well come on, Andre – let's have a look at the bracelet – there's a darling!

ANDRE: O.K. O.K. But I shall dislike it – just on principle!

The shop door opens.

ANDRE: Leave the door open, my darling. We shall not be staying very long.

WILSON: (*Polite: rather precise and prim*) Good afternoon, madam. Good afternoon, sir. And what can I have the pleasure of showing you?

ANDRE: (*Not too pleasant*) My wife insists on seeing that diamond bracelet – the one in the window – the one for which you ask the ridiculous price of two hundred guineas.

WILSON: (*With a little laugh*) It's quite an exceptional bracelet, sir – I assure you.

ANDRE: It's quite an exceptional amount of money, my friend. However ... do you mind?

WILSON: A pleasure, sir. Excuse me, madam.

We hear the sound of a showcase being opened.

LUCILLE: (*Quietly – aside*) Now don't quibble, Andre – remember this isn't Paris.

ANDRE: I know, my sweet – and remember, please, I'm not exactly made of money!

WILSON: (*Almost with reverence*) There we are, madam – isn't it perfectly exquisite? Oh, do try it on, madam – please!

LUCILLE: (*After a moment – thrilled*) Oh, Andre, isn't it lovely!

ANDRE: (*Indifferent*) M'm – M'm. So – so ... so – so, my darling.

WILSON: (*Apparently thrilled*) Excuse me, sir – but – but aren't you Monsieur d'Arnell – Monsieur Andre d'Arnell the famous detective?

ANDRE: But of course.

WILSON: I thought I recognised you, sir. I've seen your photograph so <u>many</u> times in the newspapers – Oh, really this – this is <u>quite</u> an honour, sir.

ANDRE: (*Flattered*) Tut – tut – tut … delighted, my friend. Delighted!

LUCILLE: (*Sweetly*) It's a lovely bracelet, Andre.

ANDRE: Pardon? Oh! Oh – the bracelet! (*Completely off-hand*) Take it, my darling! Take it!

In the background can be heard the sound of a motor car drawing to a standstill.

WILSON: Thank you, sir. We'll accept a cheque, Monsieur d'Arnell, so if you would care to … (*He stops talking rather suddenly*)

ANDRE: What is it? What are you staring at?

WILSON: (*Puzzled*) I'm looking at that motor car, sir – the one that's just drawn up in front of the shop window – surely the man …

LUCILLE: Andre, look! He's got something in his hand! Why – why it looks to me like …

ANDRE: (*Quickly; dramatically*) Get down!!! Get down, Lucille!! Get behind the counter!!!

We hear the smashing of glass: the spraying of machine gun bullets, followed in rapid succession by quick acceleration of a departing car and the noise of a gathering crowd.

ANDRE: Lucille! Lucille, are you all right?

LUCILLE: Yes – yes, I'm all right, Andre – but – but – but what happened?

ANDRE: I'm afraid my darling we witnessed, at rather close quarters, what is generally described as a – as a grab and smash.

LUCILLE: Smash and grab, my sweet, but …

WILSON: (*Completely bewildered*) But – but they fired a machine gun – I – I – I heard the bullets, I – I

315

quite distinctly heard the bullets. Why – why …

ANDRE: (*Amused*) Only blanks, my friend. An old trick, just to frighten us away from the window!

LUCILLE: Just look what they've done!

ANDRE: My word, they seem to have helped themselves, don't they?

WILSON: But – but who would do such a thing? Did – did you see the man, Monsieur d'Arnell? Did you catch a glimpse of …

ANDRE: No! No, I did not see him – not sufficiently well to recognise him – but there is only one man in Liverpool who would attempt such – such an outrageous escapade! His name is Consoler – Charlie Consoler. (*Thoughtfully: quite happy at the turn of events*) Lucille, my darling, I think we will pay Monsieur Consoler an unexpected visit. What do you say? (*START FADE*) But put your hat straight, my sweet – you look exactly like a turkey!

FADE.

FADE UP background noises of a fairly crowded bar parlour.

LUCILLE: Is that Mr Consoler – in the corner, Andre?

ANDRE: Yes, that's Charlie – quite a tough looking customer, isn't he, my sweet? Looks quite prosperous too. Come along, darling – let's see what he's got to say for himself.

Slightly FADE background noises.

ANDRE: Hello, Charlie.

CHARLIE: (*A tough Cockney – astonished*) Why, 'ello, guv'nor! Didn't expect to see you in this part o' the world. (*Cheery*) Sit down, guv! Sit down! What'll you 'ave?

316

ANDRE:	I'll have a few moments of your valuable time, my friend – if you have no objection?
CHARLIE:	Sure! Anything you like, Frenchy! (*Brightly*) Is this the old dragon?
ANDRE:	He means you, my sweet.
LUCILLE:	Well – really!
ANDRE:	(*Slowly*) Charlie – have you seen the newspapers this evening?
CHARLIE:	Sure! Just been readin' 'em. Blimey, bit of a smash an' grab in Cracy Street, wasn't it? Oo – they must 'ave got away with murder! What time did it 'appen, guv'nor?
ANDRE:	It happened at about half past three, my friend. (*Slowly*) Where were you at – at half past three?
CHARLIE:	Me? (*Staggered*) You – you don't think I 'ad anything to do with that lot, why … (*Laughing*) Cor blimey, you can count me out, Frenchy! I was at the League match: Liverpool versus Arsenal: wouldn't 'ave missed it for worlds! (*With enthusiasm*) You should 'ave seen the centre forward, Frenchy! From the blinkin' word go he 'ad the rest o' the …
ANDRE:	(*Interrupting CHARLIE*) What time did it start, Charlie – this – this football match?
CHARLIE:	Three o'clock – an' I was there at the kick-off. You ask Billy Norman …
ANDRE:	And you left the football match at – er?
CHARLIE:	Just after five; we 'ung abaht a bit. (*Suddenly – rather nasty*) Look 'ere, Frenchy, if you don't think I'm telling the truth then …

317

ANDRE: (*Slowly – with emphasis*) I know you are not telling the truth, my friend – and take your hand off that bottle or I shall be compelled to …

We hear the noise of d'ARNELL striking CHARLIE, who gives a cry and falls across a table which collapses.

LUCILLE: (*Shocked*) Andre! Andre, you've knocked him cold!

ANDRE: Of course I've knocked him cold, my sweet! I'm hot stuff on this knocking cold business!

LUCILLE: But – but how did you know that – that he wasn't telling the truth!

ANDRE: But it was so obvious, my sweetie-pie!!! So obvious!

FADE UP of music.
FADE DOWN.

ANNOUNCER: What made Andre d'Arnell suspect Charlie Consoler? Do you know? Later in the programme we shall return you to tonight's detective problem.

Turn over for the solution to mystery six.

MYSTERY SIX – THE SOLUTION

ANNOUNCER: We now return you to Andre d'Arnell for the solution to tonight's detective problem.

ANDRE: Of course I've knocked him cold, my sweet! I'm hot stuff on this knocking cold business!

LUCILLE: But – but how did you know that – that he wasn't telling the truth!

ANDRE: But it was so obvious, my sweetie-pie!!! So obvious!

LUCILLE: I don't see how it was obvious, Andre – after all – I never noticed it!

ANDRE: You never do notice anything, my darling! Except of course – er – the diamond bracelets!

LUCILLE: (*Not convinced*) Now look here, Andre, if he was at the football match until …

ANDRE: Lucille, my sweet, did you not hear what he said? He said that he was at a League match – Liverpool versus Arsenal. But under wartime regionalisation of League Football, Liverpool could not play Arsenal, my darling, not in a League match! Liverpool is in the League North, and Arsenal is in the League South!

LUCILLE: Andre, you're wonderful!

ANDRE: I know my sweet.

LUCILLE: You're marvellous!

ANDRE: I know my darling!

LUCILLE: You're an absolute genius!

ANDRE: Thank you my love.

LUCILLE: Andre … can I have that bracelet?

ANDRE: But, of course, my sweetie pie!
FADE UP of music.

MYSTERY SEVEN
Cast:

Andre d'Arnell . . . . Kenneth Kent

Lucille . . . . .Linden Travers

Count Leo Faranzo . . . . . Alexander Sarner

324

ANDRE: Good evening. This is Andre d'Arnell. And once again I have the pleasure of presenting to you another detective problem – a problem taken from my personal memoirs. Now listen carefully, very, very carefully my friends and see if you, too, can discover the mistake that the criminal made. (*After a moment*) One morning, two or three weeks ago, I received a letter. It was from an old friend of mine – Count Leo Faranzo. I met Leo, for the first time, in Antwerp early in 1931. A few years later he left the Continent and made his home somewhere in Cornwall. I was rather surprised to receive the letter because (*START FADE*) I had not heard from Leo for some considerable time and I distinctly remember saying to Lucille that ...

FADE.

FADE UP ANDRE.

ANDRE: Darling! Do you remember Count Faranzo?

LUCILLE: Isn't he a little man with rather prominent teeth? We met him on the Queen Mary?

ANDRE: We did not meet him on the Queen Mary, my sweetie-pie. I met him many years ago – he's tall and dignified and – and rather conceited.

LUCILLE: Conceited!

ANDRE: Yes, my sweetheart – conceited! – and don't look at me like that!

LUCILLE: Well, what's happened to the old boy – is he dead?

ANDRE:	Now, darling, don't be stupid! How could he be dead? He's just written me a letter. A most – (*Slowly*) – a most interesting letter. (*Suddenly*) And don't say: "What's happened to the <u>old</u> <u>boy</u>!" It's most undignified. Remember Count Faranzo comes from a very, very, old family – very old.
LUCILLE:	Practically decrepit.
ANDRE:	Lucille, there's no need to be … (*He stops dead*)
LUCILLE:	(*Quietly, seriously*) What is it, Andre?
ANDRE:	(*Slowly*) I'm just reading the letter, my sweetheart. Leo wants us to go down to Cornwall almost immediately. Apparently … apparently he's in some kind of … of danger.
LUCILLE:	(*START FADE on this speech and COMPLETE FADE quickly*) But, Andre, we can't possibly go down to Cornwall at a moment's notice like this! Good gracious me it would take …

FADE SCENE.

FADE UP FARANZO.

FARANZO:	(*A slow, dignified Austrian*) It's a great pleasure to see you again, Andre. You look very well, my friend. Perhaps a little stouter – yes?
ANDRE:	Stouter! It's this suit! I told you, Lucille! Brown always makes me look stout and – and pompous!
LUCILLE:	(*Laughing*) Don't be silly, Andre!
FARANZO:	(*Chuckling*) Just the same! Just as conceited as ever! Why, even in the old days, Mrs d'Arnell, he used to be so conceited that it was impossible to …

326

ANDRE: (*Interrupting FARANZO – seriously*) You did not get me down to Cornwall to talk about my conceit – nor about the past, my friend. It's the future that you are concerned with. (*Slowly*) What's troubling you, Leo?

FARANZO: (*After a moment's pause – worried*) I don't know, Andre. Strange things are happening to me these days. So strange that I ... well, let me tell you. When I bought this place seven years ago the local inhabitants here – in this village – were not exactly ... er ... were not exactly friendly. To be frank they rather resented my presence here. Gradually, however, they realised that – although I was a foreigner – I was not entirely an uncivilised sort of person. During the past three or four years we've got along rather well together. About a month ago, however, I received an anonymous letter. A rude, threatening sort of letter, and I took no notice of it. Then something happened. An attempt was made on my life – fortunately for me it failed. Two days ago, however ... the attempt was repeated.

LUCILLE: But – but haven't you any idea who's responsible? Surely ...

FARANZO: I – I have my suspicions of course, but ...

ANDRE: Whom do you suspect, Leo?

FARANZO: A man by the name of Dakar. Tom Dakar. He's a poacher. A rough, uncultured sort of chap. Lives in the village. I had a great deal of trouble with Dakar the first week I arrived here.

ANDRE: Oh?

FARANZO: Yes. He was behaving rather badly to one of my tenants – I made him – well – change his attitude – towards her. Also I had to put up an electric fence – to stop the cattle from getting onto the main road. Late one afternoon Dakar was prowling about – obviously poaching – and he nearly walked into it: fortunately he spotted the sign which I had had erected or believe me he'd have received a pretty nasty shock. But he was so angry! So angry! (*Almost amused*) Entirely overlooked the fact that he was trespassing.

ANDRE: M'm. Leo, tell me, have you that letter – the one you spoke about?

FARANZO: Yes. Yes, here it is.

ANDRE: (*Slowly*) Oh, yes.

LUCILLE: Not very well written, is it, Andre?

ANDRE: (*Thoughtfully*) He – I should say the person who wrote this letter was obviously a rough – uncultured – sort of man.

FARANZO: Oh, but Tom Dakar didn't write that letter – that's the extraordinary part about it!

ANDRE: No?

FARANZO: No, you see – when I received the letter I was so angry that I immediately went down to the village and had a word with Dakar. I told him that I thought that he'd written the letter and that I intended to communicate with the police.

ANDRE: And what happened?

FARANZO: He just laughed at me, Andre. Told me to go straight ahead. You see, the fellow's illiterate.

LUCILLE: Illiterate!

FARANZO: That's what he said, so he couldn't very well have written it, now could he?

LUCILLE: (*Laughing*) Hardly.

328

ANDRE:	(*Slowly*) Nevertheless, I've got a shrewd suspicion that he was lying to you, my friend – and that he did write that letter.
FARANZO:	But – but what makes you think that?
ANDRE:	(*Amused*) Don't you know what makes me think it, Leo? Don't you know?
LUCILLE:	(*Faintly irritated*) Andre, what are you smiling at?
ANDRE:	I'm smiling, my sweetie-pie, because it's really (*Almost a confidential whisper*) really so very, very simple …
FARANZO:	Now look here, Andre! If you're pulling my leg about this business I shall …
ANDRE:	I'm not pulling your leg, my friend. Oh, no! Oh, no!

FADE UP of music.
FADE DOWN.

ANNOUNCER:	Why does Andre d'Arnell suspect Tom Dakar? Do you know? Later in the programme you will hear from Andre d'Arnell himself the solution to tonight's detective problem.

MYSTERY SEVEN – THE SOLUTION

ANNOUNCER: We now return you to Andre d'Arnell for the solution to tonight's detective problem.

FARANZO: Now look here, Andre! If you're pulling my leg about this business I shall …

ANDRE: I'm not pulling your leg, my friend. Oh, no! Oh, no! Don't you remember what happened when Tom Dakar almost walked into the electric fence?

FARANZO: (*Puzzled*) What do you mean?

LUCILLE: I don't understand, Andre?

ANDRE: You never do understand, darling. However, permit me to elucidate. Tom Dakar was out poaching – he almost – <u>almost</u> – walked into the electric fence.

FARANZO: Well?

ANDRE: Well, why didn't he walk into the electric fence? Why – why <u>almost</u>? What exactly made our friend hesitate?

FARANZO: (*Impatiently*) I've told you, Andre! He read the notice that I … (*He stops*)

ANDRE: (*Slowly*) He read the notice warning people not to go near the fence! Correct?

FARANZO: (*Staggered*) Why – why, yes!

LUCILLE: (*Suddenly seeing the point*) But – but how could he read the notice if – if he's illiterate!

ANDRE: (*Pulling LUCILLE's leg*) Why, Lucille, my sweet – you're, you're wonderful. You're superb! You're, you're magnifique!

330

LUCILLE: (*Conceitedly – imitating ANDRE*) Thank you, my sweetie-pie!

ANDRE: (*Taken by surprise*) Oh! Oh! La! La!

FADE UP of music.

MYSTERY EIGHT
Cast:

Andre d'Arnell . . . . Kenneth Kent

Lucille . . . . .Linden Travers

Sergeant . . . . .Fred Yule

Sharpe . . . . Cyril Gardiner

As the opening music finishes CROSS FADE to d'ARNELL.

ANDRE: Good evening, my friends. How are you all this evening? Well, tonight I want you to listen very carefully to my detective problem and see if you, too, like Andre d'Arnell, can discover the mistake that the criminal made. (*After a moment*) One night – it was a week ago last Wednesday to be precise – Lucille and I had a most interesting experience. We were returning to London, after our trip to Cornwall, and we had passed through the little town of Tavistock when (*START FADE*) suddenly Lucille turned towards me and said …

FADE.

CROSS FADE to the sound of a car at cruising speed.

LUCILLE: Andre!

ANDRE: Yes, my darling?

LUCILLE: Do you see that light … look! … on the road about fifty yards ahead …

ANDRE: (*Peering*) Yes, and I hope it's a garage, Lucille. I need some water for the … (*Suddenly*) Why, it's the police, my sweet. They must be looking for someone.

The car slows down and draws to a standstill.

SERGEANT: (*A slight West country accent – brisk manner*) Good evening, sir.

ANDRE: Good evening, sergeant!

SERGEANT: I'd just like to take a look in the back of the car, sir – if you don't mind.

ANDRE: Go ahead, my friend!

The car door opens.

335

ANDRE:	(*After a moment*) What are you looking for – the Crown Jewels?
SERGEANT:	No, sir. Escaped convict. Gent by the name of George Hensford. Nice, slippery sort o' customer too, if you be asking me.
LUCILLE:	When did he escape, Sergeant – this afternoon?
SERGEANT:	No, ma'am – this morning soon after breakfast. Leading us a proper dance 'e be an' no mistake. (*Dismissing the d'ARNELLs*) That's o.k., sir.
ANDRE:	Thank you, my friend. (*Suddenly*) Oh – where can I get some water for the radiator? Is there a garage on this road?
SERGEANT:	Not for a mile or two, sir. There's a house up on top of the hill – Dr Sharpe – the doctor'll give you a jug of water with pleasure, if he's in, sir.
ANDRE:	Thank you, Sergeant.
SERGEANT:	Goodnight, sir. Goodnight ma'am.
LUCILLE:	Goodnight.

We hear the sound of the car starting and gathering speed.
FADE.

FADE UP the noise of the car ticking over.
The car door opens and closes.

LUCILLE:	Oh, that's better. (*Stretching herself*) I was getting so cramped in the car.

FADE the car completely.
We hear the noise of footsteps on gravel.

ANDRE:	This must be the house, Lucille, but there doesn't appear to be a light of any sort!
LUCILLE:	Oh dear. It's starting to rain!

ANDRE: Come along, we'll see if we can make anyone …

LUCILLE: (*Suddenly, very startled*) Andre!

ANDRE: (*Tensely*) What is it?

LUCILLE: (*Slowly – tense*) Andre, I thought I saw someone … up at that top window … staring at us … staring as if …

ANDRE: Now don't start imagining things, my sweetie-pie! (*Suddenly*) Ah, here's the bell.

We hear the sound of the bell being pulled and the sound of an old-fashioned bell clangs in the background.

LUCILLE: There doesn't appear to be anyone in, Andre. And yet I'm sure …

ANDRE: (*Quickly*) Sh!

We hear the noise of the door being unbolted and the door opens.

SHARPE: (*Quite a pleasant voice – very sure of himself*) Good evening …

ANDRE: Good evening. I'm so sorry to trouble you, but could I possibly have a little water for my car? The radiator seems to be …

SHARPE: Why, yes, of course. Do come in. Do come in, sir. T't – t't – what a wretched night to be sure!

The door closes.

SHARPE: I don't suppose you happen to be going on to Okehampton by any chance, sir?

ANDRE: Why, yes – as a matter of fact we are.

LUCILLE: We thought of staying the night there.

SHARPE: Oh, this is indeed providential! I wonder, sir – could I possibly beg a lift into Okehampton? I had a telephone call through from a patient of mine a few minutes ago, and … oh, forgive me, my name is Sharpe, Dr Wesley Sharpe.

ANDRE:	Delighted to be of service, doctor.
LUCILLE:	(*Quietly*) Doctor, is there anyone else in the house at the moment, besides yourself?
SHARPE:	(*Surprised*) Why, no. I have a housekeeper, of course, but she happens to be away for a (*Hesitantly*) day or two. (*Puzzled*) Why do you ask?
LUCILLE:	Well …
ANDRE:	My wife thought she saw someone when we came down the drive. Someone – someone staring at us from one of the bedroom windows.
SHARPE:	That's quite impossible, I assure you, sir. There's no one upstairs. I've been down here all the evening reading Somerset Maugham's book The Razor's Edge. As a matter of fact the only thing that took my mind off that interesting character Harry was ITMA, which I was listening to when …
ANDRE:	Excuse me, doctor, but if you'll get the water we shall be delighted to take you into Okehampton.
SHARPE:	Oh, thank you, sir. My own car happens to be in dock at the moment, so this is a great help! Do sit down, dear lady. Do sit down.

A door opens.

SHARPE:	I shan't keep you waiting long, sir.

The door closes.

LUCILLE:	He seems quite a pleasant … Andre, what are you doing? (*Surprised*) Are you going to use the telephone?
ANDRE:	(*Faintly pleased with himself*) No. No, I'm just looking at it, my sweetie-pie!

LUCILLE:	Just looking at it! (*Quickly, sensing that all is not well*) Andre! Andre, what's the matter?
ANDRE:	Sh!

The door opens.

SHARPE:	Well, here's the water, sir – so if you'll just attend to the car while …
ANDRE:	(*Interrupting SHARPE – quite pleasant*) Doctor, what is your telephone number here?
SHARPE:	My – my telephone number?
ANDRE:	Yes.
SHARPE:	Why, it's – (*With a little laugh*) – it's on the telephone.
ANDRE:	Yes, I know it's on the telephone, my friend – but what is the number?
SHARPE:	It's – er – er – Tavistock – er – (*Suddenly*) Look here, what are you suggesting, sir?
ANDRE:	I am suggesting, my friend, that you don't even know the number.
LUCILLE:	But he's bound to know his own telephone number, Andre. Why …
ANDRE:	You would think so – wouldn't you, my sweet?
SHARPE:	What are you getting at?
ANDRE:	I am getting at the fact, monsieur, that you are not Dr Sharpe!!
SHARPE:	(*Angry – much commoner voice*) Who are you? What do you want?
ANDRE:	My name is d'Arnell! Andre d'Arnell!! And you, unless I'm greatly mistaken, monsieur, are the escaped convict – George Hensford!!
LUCILLE:	But, Andre …
ANDRE:	Stand still, my friend, or you may get hurt.
SHARPE:	How did you know?

FADE UP of music.

FADE DOWN.

ANNOUNCER: What made Andre d'Arnell suspect the doctor? Do you know? Later in the programme we shall return you to Andre d'Arnell for the solution to tonight's detective problem.

Sadly the solution to mystery eight no longer exists but can you solve the mystery as you think Andre d'Arnell did?

MYSTERY NINE
Cast:
Andre d'Arnell . . . . Kenneth Kent

Lucille . . . . .Linden Travers

As the opening music finishes CROSS FADE to d'ARNELL.

ANDRE: Good evening, my friends. I wonder if you have noticed how sometimes the most exciting things happen so – so suddenly? What you call in this country – out of the blue. Late one night a few weeks ago, Lucille and I had – to say the least – a most unusual experience. We had been away for the weekend and it was about half past eleven at night when we arrived home. I had an extremely bad cold in the head and I was (*START FADE*) feeling, to be quite frank, rather disgruntled with myself. I remember saying to Lucille that …

FADE.

FADE UP ANDRE.

ANDRE: (*Faintly irritated*) Have you rung for the lift, my sweet?

LUCILLE: Yes, but nothing seems to be happening. I'll try again.

ANDRE: T't! T't! This is going to be pleasant, I must say – climbing six flights of stairs with a heavy suitcase! (*Irritated*) Darling, when we go away for the weekend why do you have to take your complete wardrobe!

LUCILLE: Don't be silly, Andre – I only took four dresses.

ANDRE: Four dresses for two days! You women! You change your dresses almost as often as you change your minds. (*Petulantly*) What is the matter with this lift!!

LUCILLE: Darling, don't be petulant! You can see what's the matter. Someone's forgotten to close the gate, that's all. The lift's at the first floor – look!

345

ANDRE: (*Peering*) Oh, yes … yes, of course! How inconsiderate! Come along, Lucille, we'd better …

LUCILLE: No, you wait here with the case. I'll slip upstairs and come down in the lift.

LUCILLE starts to ascend the stairs.

ANDRE: O.K. O.K., Lucille. (*He commences to sing to himself. He breaks off and sneezes*) T't, this dreadful cold!

We hear a terrified shriek from LUCILLE.

LUCILLE: (*From the first floor: desperate*) Andre! Andre!

ANDRE: (*Tensely*) What is it, Lucille? What is it?

LUCILLE: Quickly! Come quickly!

ANDRE: Coming, Lucille! I'm coming!!

ANDRE ascends the stairs.

ANDRE: (*Out of breath*) Lucille, what on earth is all the excitem … (*He stops dead*)

LUCILLE: (*Staring – tensely*) Look at that girl, Andre – in – the – lift. Look – look at the blood all over … all over … (*Gives a little frightened cry of horror*)

ANDRE: (*Softly – still tense*) Take a grip on yourself, Lucille! Now stay where you are, darling.

LUCILLE: (*After a moment – softly*) Is – is she dead?

ANDRE: Yes – she's been dead about half an hour I should say – stabbed to death. Look … here's the knife …

LUCILLE: (*Horrified*) Oh – oh, Andre, I'm – I'm going to faint!

ANDRE: (*Very business-like*) Not now, my darling – we haven't time for fainting! Wait here! I'm going downstairs to the telephone in the hall. (*START FADE*) And as soon as I can get in touch with the …

FADE.

FADE UP LUCILLE.

LUCILLE: Well, how are you feeling, Andre?

ANDRE: (*Extremely sorry for himself*) Oh, I feel – I feel (*He sneezes*) I feel terrible, my darling! And just look at me! I look like an old man with a long white beard!

LUCILLE: Don't be so conceited, Andre!

ANDRE: Darling, I'm not conceited! You know jolly well I'm not really conceited – it's only a joke to – what do you say? – pull your leg!

LUCILLE: (*With a laugh*) Yes, Andre, I know – but just at the moment you're not looking exactly pleased with yourself.

ANDRE: I'm not feeling very pleased with myself, darling. After all, don't forget I've been in bed for two whole days – for two whole days, Lucille – and there's a murder waiting to be investigated right under my very nose. (*With emotional emphasis*) Right under my very nose.

LUCILLE: Andre! Remember your temperature!

ANDRE: M'm – well, what have <u>you</u> been doing with yourself this last two or three days?

LUCILLE: (*Nervously*) I've – now don't laugh, Andre! – I've been investigating.

ANDRE: Investigating! (*With a little laugh*) Investigating what?

LUCILLE: The – the murder …

ANDRE: (*Astonished and amused*) Oh? So? Oh, this is most interesting. So you have been investigating the murder, my sweetie-pie.

LUCILLE: (*Taking herself very seriously*) Yes, I – I've found out that the girl – the one we found in the lift – works, or rather worked, at Cranston's the

347

florists in New Bond Street. Her name was Betty Maine. She appears to have been …

ANDRE: (*Interrupting LUCILLE on the word 'street'*) Very clever of you, Lucille. Very clever! But I suppose you know that all these interesting details were in the newspapers this morning?

LUCILLE: Yes, Andre, I know all about that. But here's something that wasn't in the newspapers. Although Betty Maine was married she was separated from her husband and was friendly with a man by the name of Brian Cardwell. He has a flat in this building. Now Cardwell was getting rather tired of Miss Maine and according to rumours had …

ANDRE: (*Suddenly taking notice*) How do you know that she was friendly with this man Cardwell?

LUCILLE: (*Slowly*) Andre, you're – you're not going to be angry with me – are you, my sweet?

ANDRE: (*Watching LUCILLE*) What do you mean?

LUCILLE: Do you remember … after we discovered the body … you – you went downstairs to telephone?

ANDRE: Well?

LUCILLE: Well, I – I pulled myself together and I … I … (*Gives a reassuring little laugh*) I – er –

ANDRE: (*Slowly*) You …. WHAT … Lucille?

LUCILLE: I searched the body. I found this diary, Andre – that's how I know about … Brian Cardwell.

ANDRE: (*Amazed*) Well, to think that … (*Suddenly – intrigued*) Go on, Lucille. Go on. Have you seen this man Cardwell?

LUCILLE: Yes, I saw him this morning – and the – er – husband.

348

ANDRE: So? Quite the Criminal Investigator, Lucille! And what did they say?

LUCILLE: Well, they both appear to have been out of Town when the murder was committed – which, as you know, was about eleven o'clock on Monday night. Cardwell went down to Cambridge for the weekend. He says he goes down there quite a lot to see a friend of his at the University.

ANDRE: What time did he arrive at Cambridge, do you know?

LUCILLE: Yes, about half past ten in the morning – this was on the Saturday. He came back to Town on Tuesday afternoon.

ANDRE: Did he stay with this friend of his?

LUCILLE: No. No, I don't think so. The friend's at Brasenose College, but they saw a great deal of each other.

ANDRE: And what about the husband, Lucille? How does he strike you?

LUCILLE: I don't know. He's a cameraman down at Elstree. At least he says he is. Apparently, he spent the weekend at Birmingham. Went down to see a film – Noel Coward's This Happy Breed. He says he very badly wanted to see the film and unfortunately missed it when it was in Town.

ANDRE: Well, I hope it met with his approval!

LUCILLE: It seems to have done so. He thought the technicolour was first rate. (*After a moment*) You know, Andre, I feel quite sure that one of them – either Brian Cardwell or the husband …

ANDRE: You feel quite sure that one of them is not exactly telling the truth, eh, Lucille? (*Laughing*) But, of course one of them is not telling the truth, my sweetie-pie! Oh, and it's so simple!

349

LUCILLE: (*Astounded*) Why, Andre, I fail to see how on earth you can possibly say that it's …

FADE UP of music.
FADE DOWN.

ANNOUNCER: Who does Andre d'Arnell suspect? Do you know? Later in the programme we shall return you to Andre d'Arnell for the solution to tonight's detective problem.

Turn over the page for the solution to mystery nine.

MYSTERY NINE – THE SOLUTION

ANNOUNCER: We now return you to Andre d'Arnell for the solution to tonight's detective problem.

LUCILLE: (*Astounded*) Why, Andre, I fail to see how on earth you can possibly say that it's …

ANDRE: Now listen, my darling. He's told you – this Monsieur Cardwell – that he was in Cambridge.

LUCILLE: That's right, Andre. He went down to Cambridge on Saturday and came back to Town on Tuesday afternoon.

ANDRE: That is, in fact, his alibi. That he visited a friend of his who is studying at Brasenose College, Cambridge.

LUCILLE: That's right, Andre.

ANDRE: Think, my sweet-pie!

LUCILLE: What do you mean?

ANDRE: Think, my sweetheart!

LUCILLE: (*Suddenly*) Andre! Andre! Brasenose College isn't at Cambridge – it's at Oxford!

ANDRE: (*Laughing*) That's just the point, Lucille!

LUCILLE: (*Childishly delighted*) And I saw it!

ANDRE: Yes – you saw it, my – my beautiful detective!

LUCILLE: (*Pleased with herself*) There you are, Andre! Now what have you got that I haven't got?

ANDRE: This wretched cold, my sweetie-pie! (*He sneezes*)

FADE UP of music.